MW00522689

The high-compression stories in Peter Johnson's hyper-readable *Shot* open in 4th gear and accelerate from there. Take "Pretty Girl" which begins: "So you ask, 'How could anyone so drop-dead gorgeous be afraid of mirrors?'" The considerable underlying art in these stories is matched by their fresh energy and flat-out fun. What this book has in common with Johnson's poetry is his insistence that a writer gets down more than craft, that a work of art also entertain.

—Stuart Dybek, MacArthur fellow
and author of *The Coast of Chicago* and *I Sailed with Magellan*

Nobody knows the dark chemistry of relationships better than Peter Johnson. In these gripping tales, Johnson gets right down to the real nitty gritty. Love, hate, fear. All the elements of great fiction, in the hands of a master storyteller. Stories that will forever beat in the American heart.

—*Rod Philbrick*, Newbery Honor recipient and author of *Freak the Mighty*

Peter Johnson hits the bullseye with this memorable collection of linked short stories that examines the impact of a fatal shooting on a group of surviving teens. The dead-on results, both thought-provoking and compelling, will appeal equally to teen and adult readers.

—Michael Cart, Booklist columnist and author of *From Romance to Realism: Fifty Years of Growth and Change in Young Adult Literature*

In this novel, told from multiple points of view, critically acclaimed and award-winning author Peter Johnson paints a nuanced and convincing portrait of teenagers whose lives are forever changed—and linked—by the sound of a single gunshot. Johnson never apologizes for his characters' thoughts or actions, and therein lies this novel's brilliance. The brutal honesty and lack of self-reflection with which the narrators speak ring true and provide penetrating insights into the insecurity and insensitivity that permeate our lives. We are not only left wondering how we have created a society that continues to condone tremendous violence against women, but, like Maura, we are also left asking why we allow and even encourage people—especially young men—to remain irresponsible and uncaring.

—PADMA VENKATRAMAN, author of *The Bridge Home*
and *Climbing the Stairs*

Peter Johnson's braided and bangled cable knot collection of connected stories, *Shot*, has Zeno Double-Dutching with Heraclitus, jumping into the same river more than twice in this swing dance of string theory. Meticulous. Marvelous. The scalloping plots plot a chorus line of ouroboros, buoyant breech-loaded backtracking. This book is an intricately unfolding map more detailed than the thing it represents, saturated and satisfying.

—MICHAEL MARTONE, author of *The Moon
over Wapakoneta* and *Brooding*

Johnson's stories are smart, deft, and funny, not to mention as potent as a bullet to the brain.

—E. C. OSONDU, Caine Prize Winner, author of *Voice of America*

SHOT:
A NOVEL IN STORIES

For Dylan:
Hope you enjoy this
quirky book. It will
be my favorite.
Keep reading & be
good to your cool mom.
Peter

S H O T :
A N O V E L I N S T O R I E S

Peter Johnson

Peter Johnson

MADHAT PRESS
CHESHIRE, MASSACHUSETTS

MadHat Press
MadHat Incorporated
PO Box 422, Cheshire, MA 01225

The Library of Congress has assigned
this edition a Control Number of
2021939146

ISBN 978-1-952335-24-2 (paperback)

Text by Peter Johnson
Cover design by Marc Vincenz

www.madhat-press.com

First Printing
Printed in the United States of America

Other Books by Peter Johnson

Prose Poetry

Pretty Happy!

Miracles & Mortifications

Eduardo & "I"

Rants and Raves: Selected and New Prose Poems

Old Man Howling at the Moon

Love Poems for the Millennium

Young Adult/Adult

What Happened

Loserville

Out of Eden

I'm a Man: Short Stories

Middle Grade

The Amazing Adventures of John Smith Jr., AKA Houdini

The Life and Times of Benny Alvarez

The Night Before Krampus

Essays

Truths, Falsehoods, and a Wee Bit of Honesty: A Short Primer on the Prose Poem With Selected Letters from Russell Edson

For Rod Philbrick and Joe Monninger

Table of Contents

Ghost stories written as algebraic equations. Little Emily at the blackboard is very frightened. The X's look like a graveyard at night. The teacher wants her to poke among them with a piece of chalk. All the children hold their breath. The white chalk squeaks once among the plus and minus signs, and then it's quiet again.

—Charles Simic, from *The World Doesn't End*

If a book doesn't begin with "A shot rang out," I don't want to read it.

—Kingsley Amis

THE GUNSLINGER

The gray minivan reeked of cigarettes and fear.

The cigarettes belonged to Maura's mother, but the fear was hers.

She turned the key and the engine coughed itself awake. The late afternoon sun—still hot—flashed menacingly off the hood.

Maura was going to buy a gun.

Unlike her friend Gabby, Maura knew nothing about guns, but just last summer Gabby had told her how a carload of boys had peppered her housing project with bullets while neighbors were outside barbecuing and making small talk. Gabby also said she knew where to get a gun if Maura ever felt threatened, which was why Maura was picking her up.

It was a short drive to the Dunkin' Donuts located at one end of a strip mall. Maura could see Gabby standing on the corner, yelling at two guys in a yellow Mustang convertible. She wore skin-tight jeans and a snug white sleeveless top, her dark henna-colored hair drawn back into a ponytail. She was tall and lean, her body sculpted from exercise and weight training. She was a sprinter. That's how she and Maura had met last summer—Gabby sprinting the 100- and 200-meter dashes, and Maura running long distance. Neither of them could afford a premier track camp, so their coaches finagled them scholarships. They practiced together for four weeks that summer and kept in touch through Facebook, sometimes meeting at the mall for lunch.

Maura pulled up behind the Mustang. When Gabby saw her, she shot the guys in the car the finger, and one of them called her a slut before they peeled away.

"Slut, my ass," Gabby said, sliding into the front seat of the minivan. Maura laughed.

"It's not funny. These dumb boys think every cute girl has the morals of a rap diva. I'm a straight-A student on the fast track to something big."

There was little doubt in Maura's mind that Gabby was right about that. She was about to pull back onto the highway when Gabby grabbed her by the forearm and said, "Girl, why did you scrub yourself down?"

"What?"

"No makeup. You look like a nun."

Maura felt herself smile, and that was nice, because for the last few weeks she had been so depressed that she'd had trouble getting out of bed. And as for makeup, the truth was, she didn't want to look pretty anymore.

"Don't worry about today," Gabby said. "These guys will want your money, and then we're gone. They don't need information. You understand?"

Maura nodded.

"No need to share. You want protection, right? You said the guy might hurt you."

Maura nodded again.

"You're not going to do anything stupid, right?"

"No," Maura said.

* * *

Alex didn't think much about it when he first saw Maura at the mall. He needed new desert boots. They were $150, but he needed them, so his mother gave him the money. It was nice to be able to spend money like that and not have to work crappy summer jobs to buy clothes. Instead, he had time to work out or to play *Grand Theft Auto* or to watch porn.

As he was leaving the shoe store, he saw her sitting in the food court on a bench by a water fountain. Looking at him. Not waving or approaching, just staring. He waved, but she didn't respond, so he kept walking toward J. Crew. He needed new shorts and some T-shirts. He needed some kind of lightweight pants.

After he left J. Crew he saw her a second time, perched on the edge of another bench across from the store. Now this was getting annoying.

She actually looked good. She wore white short shorts and a blue sleeveless knit top, her long brown hair breaking across her breasts. She had one leg crossed over the other. She had nice legs. He remembered that, and also the green pendant that hung from her neck. The night of the party, after she had overreacted, he noticed it on the floor and had slid it into her pocket. That was nice of him, he thought.

But this was creeping him out, so he decided to talk to her.

"What's up?" he said.

She kept staring at him, looking a little stoned.

"Okay," he said. "If that's the way you want it, I'm cool with that."

Still no response. She looked sad, then angry, then sad again.

"I gotta go," he said. "But let's talk sometime, okay?"

He was about to leave when she said something, very softly.

"What?" he said.

"I said, Why?"

Now *this* was awkward.

"Like I said, Maura, let's get together. Someplace quiet. But I have stuff to do now. I'll call, okay?"

Still no answer, so he smiled and headed toward the kiosk that sold sunglasses. That was the last item he wanted to buy.

He didn't see her again until after he'd paid for parking and walked through the steamy underground garage toward his red Audi, a present for turning eighteen. He wanted to get home, then go to the club for a quick dip. Dory Scheff said she'd be there around three. Dory was hot, and as far he knew, no one had gotten with her. She could be a bitch, but that was what he liked about her.

He placed a few bags on the hood while he opened the door. When he went to grab them, he spotted Maura leaning against a concrete pillar.

This was too much now. He tossed the bags into the back seat. He was going to talk to her, say it was creepy to stalk him. She had everything all wrong. If it hadn't been for him, she would've been in real trouble.

3

He looked for her again, wanting to make things right, but she was gone.

* * *

Maura was surprised where she and Gabby had ended up. She had expected a run-down neighborhood, with drug dealers and prostitutes hanging out on street corners. Instead, interspersed among yellow-brick, three-story apartment complexes were a number of well-kept two-family homes. Maura wouldn't have chosen to walk there alone at midnight, but now, at 4 p.m., kids were playing street soccer, and a gray-haired black man was smoking a pipe on a front porch.

"I thought you said you lived in the projects," Maura said to Gabby.

"Well, this ain't exactly Beverly Hills. Just remember what I said, these boys will try to spook you, so ignore them. You've got the money, right?"

"Yeah," Maura said.

Gabby led her up the stairs of a white two-family and motioned for Maura to follow her inside, where they found four boys about Maura's age. Two were on the floor playing a video game, flanked by empty beer cans. On a nearby couch, a pale, thin kid wearing mid-calf black denim shorts and a black T-shirt waved to Gabby. He was sketching the two video players on lined pages of a spiral notebook. He was good. Beside him was a kid with close-cut blond hair, who was shirtless and heavily muscled, and next to him was a shoebox.

They all stopped and stared at the girls. They looked hungry. They looked like they wanted to have fun.

When the kid with the sketchpad saw them, he was up in an instant. "Welcome," he said, jokingly bowing toward Maura.

"This is my cousin Lonny," Gabby said. "This is his house."

"You girls want somethin' to drink?" Lonny said.

Maura felt her chest tighten, but she knew she couldn't leave now.

"Just give us the gun and we'll be on our way," Gabby said.

Lonny's lips widened into a grin and he shook his finger playfully at her. "And you used to be so much fun, cousin."

"I was never fun like that," Gabby said.

"Like what?"

"Like what you mean."

The shirtless kid stood and approached, then stopped as if sizing them up. He knew he had a nice body. "No time like the present," he said. He had the blank, unfocused eyes of someone on drugs, and Maura wondered what he was capable of. She knew what happened when guys got high.

"The gun, Lonny," Gabby said. "Now, or I'll tell your mom what you've been up to."

"The money first," Lonny said, so Maura got the $100 from her purse and handed it to him.

The shirtless kid opened the shoebox and took out a gun. It was smaller than Maura expected. Her first inclination was to run, until she remembered why she was there.

The kid surprised everyone by pointing the gun at the two girls.

"Get that outta my face," Gabby said.

"It's not loaded," he said. "The bullets are in the box." He scrutinized Maura, as if she were a bug he was about to squash. "You aim to shoot someone?"

"No, just scare him," Maura said.

Maura could feel Gabby staring at her. She hadn't exactly told Gabby the truth.

"How does it work?" Maura asked.

The boys laughed, and the shirtless one said, "You point it at someone and pull the trigger."

"Yeah," one of the kids on the floor said, "or sometimes it goes off by itself. I once shot a dude in the hand by mistake."

"Yeah, a mistake," Lonny said, and they all laughed again.

"Here," the shirtless kid said. "Hold it."

Reluctantly, Maura took the gun, surprised at how light it was. Suddenly she wasn't so afraid. She felt as if she'd done this before, maybe as a kid. Maybe she'd held a toy gun, and it was as simple as that. Maybe she wouldn't even have to put bullets in it. After a few seconds, it felt warm in her hand.

"That's enough," Gabby said, looking curiously at Maura. She took

5

the gun from her and returned it to the box. "We're outta here."

Everything would've been fine except that one of the kids from the floor began to circle them. He feinted to the left, then to right, like a boxer. Then the shirtless kid did the same, poking Maura in the ribs. "Time to party," he said.

Maura remembered another room, a girl's bedroom, but not hers.

She looked at the box with the gun in it, but Gabby got there first and wedged the box under her arm. "You wannabe gangsta boys don't scare us," she said.

"Hey, hey," the shirtless kid said. "That kind of talk won't do." He was mad now. He was going to do something stupid. That's what guys did when they were mad.

Lonny got in the kid's face. "Chill out," he said, and then to Gabby, "Just scat, girl."

"You really going to let 'em go?" the shirtless kid said.

"She's family," Lonny said, and that reminder calmed everyone long enough for Maura and Gabby to move toward the front door.

In the car Gabby said, "Who're you going to scare? You said your mama's boyfriend's getting crazy. That you wanted the gun just in case."

Maura had lied about the boyfriend.

"Does it matter?" was all she could say.

"Sure does, girl," Gabby said. "I don't want you shooting up your school or something crazy like that. Don't make me sorry for helping you."

"I won't," Maura said.

"Promise?"

"Promise."

* * *

To Alex she was one of those girls you go through school never noticing. Not a geek or an outsider. Just a quiet presence, the girl barely visible at the edge of the class photo, too polite to push her way to the front. There was something sexy about that kind of shyness, so when Campbell McVeigh pointed her out, it got Alex thinking.

"Something's changing with that girl," Campbell had said.

"What girl?"

"The one by the water fountain. I think her name's Laura or Maura, something like that. Really nice legs, but I don't remember her ever wearing a skirt that short. It's something that would've registered."

The girl was sipping from the fountain, and Alex had to agree about her legs.

"Definitely a possible notch on The Gunslinger's holster," Campbell said.

That's what Alex's friends called him, The Gunslinger. He thought it was a stupid name, though it was cool to have that reputation, even if it was exaggerated. At first he thought girls would shy away when they heard about it, but the opposite seemed to be happening. Which was partly why he had approached the girl at the fountain.

She seemed startled by his presence and dropped a book onto the floor. When he picked it up, he bumped into her, and she blushed. That's when he knew it was a done deal. Just a question of how to handle it.

"Sorry," he said, smiling. "I'm a klutz."

"Not what I'd expect from a jock," she said.

So she has some spunk, Alex thought, and for the first time he looked closely at her. She was cute but, for some reason, just missed being hot. Was it her nose? Her mouth? Were her eyes too close or too far apart? He couldn't put his finger on it, couldn't figure out why she'd been easy to overlook for so many years.

"You make it sound like a disease," Alex said.

"If I thought that, I wouldn't be running cross-country and track," she said, but then she blushed again as if she wanted to take it back.

That's where I saw her, Alex thought, remembering how the cross-country team practiced on the track circling the football field.

And so they agreed to meet at the pizzeria, where they talked about school and plans she had for the future. The usual stuff Alex had to listen to, knowing he had to go slow with this girl. A few more dates and then they'd go to his cousin Henry's party. It was in another town. Most of the kids would be from Henry's private school, and Henry's parents would be in Europe, so they'd have the house to themselves.

On the third date he kissed her, not hard, teasing her with his tongue to see what she knew, which wasn't much. Her tongue tasted sweet, like mangoes or blueberries—perhaps the aftertaste from a stick of gum she'd been chewing. He never touched her while they kissed, just leaned in innocently, not wanting to scare her off. It was a nice kiss, and for a moment he wondered if he might end up liking this girl. She was different—inexperienced but a little feisty, too. He learned a lot about her: that her father had split, that she thought her mother was prettier than her (which turned out to be true), and that they were having a tough time financially. The more he learned, the more he realized how unhappy and vulnerable she was.

So he asked her to Henry's party, and she said yes. He told her to bring her bathing suit, and he promised her mother she'd be back by midnight. He did all the right things. He gave her mother Henry's address and also his own parents' phone numbers, knowing she'd never call.

So everything was set. What made it even better was that he was looking forward to the party. He was beginning to like this girl ... Maura.

* * *

Maura arranged the bullets on her bed into the shape of a fan. Although she didn't plan on shooting the gun, she practiced inserting and removing the bullets. She felt powerful while pointing the gun when the cylinders were empty, but when full, the weapon seemed heavier, as if weighed down by the possibility of death. She held it at arm's length, her hand uncontrollably shaking, which made her realize she could never actually shoot anyone. She stared at the gun, still amazed at how easy it had been to buy.

At one point, she decided to remove all but one bullet. She imagined standing over Alex, spinning the chamber, playing Russian roulette. She was about to take out that last bullet when she heard a knock. It was her mother calling her for dinner. Nervously, she placed the gun into the box and slid it under her bed.

Downstairs her mother was methodically chopping garlic for a Caesar salad. Plates of warmed-up macaroni and cheese rested on two straw placemats facing each other on the dinner table. Maura watched as her mother blended the garlic into the dressing and then dripped it onto the romaine lettuce.

Maura hadn't yet told her mother about Alex dumping her. According to her mother, because Alex was rich, he was Maura's "way out," an opportunity to have the life she deserved, which obviously wasn't the one she was currently living. Maura couldn't bear to disappoint her mother. She was sick of seeing her nod off on the couch every night while drinking a glass of cheap Chablis and watching reruns of *Beachfront Bargain Hunters*—all the time wishing she could live in those exotic locations.

Her mother turned and carried the wooden bowl of Caesar salad to the table. She was smiling as she sat down. "So what do you and Alex have planned this summer?"

Maura forced a smile in return, trying to keep her voice from cracking. A number of lies flashed through her mind. "We haven't talked much about it," she said.

Her mother reached over and touched Maura's wrist. "Whatever, it will be more exciting than what I'm doing. Oh, to be young again," she said wistfully, tossing the salad and lifting it carefully onto their plates.

After supper and back in her room, Maura thought about yesterday afternoon, wondering why she had followed Alex to the mall. How like her it was to cower in the distance instead of yelling at him. How she hated that nagging weakness she felt she had inherited from her mother. She was athletic and smart but knew that her chances of becoming one of the cool kids—the ones who seemed so confident, so unafraid—were slim to none. It wasn't as if she were ugly, and she could even be funny and witty at times, but she had never let herself get close to anyone, relaxed only when she could drift in and out of life on her own terms. To top it off, her father was AWOL and her mother dated older divorced guys who never stayed with her no matter how much she flattered them.

So Maura was surprised when Alex had asked her out, even more surprised that he was nice. She knew his reputation, but the other girls were wrong. She'd been kissed by a few boys, and Alex's kisses were sincere. She even trusted him enough to confide in him about her father and to admit that she was jealous of her mother's looks, and that, secretly, she thought her mother had driven her father away.

So how did she end up at a lousy mall, stalking him, able to mumble only one word, "Why?"

He probably laughed all the way home. She could almost hear that laugh, along with the laughter of the other boys, the ones at Lonny's house and at Henry's party. Those memories frightened her, but she wasn't going to be scared anymore.

Alex was.

* * *

If Alex were ever on trial—and he sometimes worried that Maura might bring it to that—this is what he'd say.

First, he wasn't a creep. He took only what was offered. What did Maura think they were going to do at Henry's party? Hold hands? Up until then, he had never tried to get with her, but it was only natural to take it to the next level.

The night of the party it was about eighty degrees, and everyone was drinking or smoking dope. He was surprised at how well Maura fit in, almost proud to be with her. Early on, she didn't drink, but then someone handed her a rum and Coke, and she liked it. He told her to take it easy. These weren't your normal rum and Cokes—more like glasses of rum with a shot of Coke. But Maura kept downing them, becoming more relaxed and talkative. That's when he realized his night might get more interesting if the drinks kept coming, so he mixed them himself.

But then she had to make fun of the gunslinger thing, and that pissed him off. So he led her to the greenhouse, wanting to show her who was in charge. He started to kiss her, hard, and she pushed him away, so he slowed down, regaining her trust. They made out for a while, and then he steered her out of the greenhouse through a swarm of drunken kids toward the main house, finally ending up in Henry's sister's bedroom.

Things were looking good until she said she wanted to go home, and that didn't seem fair. Rather than get mad, he was smart enough to back off. He'd been through this before. He coaxed her onto the bed and began kissing her the way he had on previous dates. She seemed okay with that and even kissed him back. But then she started to nod off, so he had to push the issue, jostling her awake until they eventually got it on.

Afterwards, she fell asleep, and while he was getting dressed, Henry and two other guys barged in.

"Whoops," Henry said.

Then one of Henry's friends said, "Seconds, anyone?" while another grabbed his phone to take a few pictures.

"Leave her alone," Alex said, reaching for the phone.

"Well, *you* certainly didn't," Henry said.

Alex got in between them and Maura.

"You'd actually get your ass kicked for her?" Henry said.

Alex looked at Maura stretched out helplessly on the bed and decided the whole thing wasn't worth a beating. "Come on, dude," he said. "Can't you see she's wasted?"

"Isn't that the point?" Henry said.

That's when one of Henry friends, a big guy with a buzz cut who looked like he played football, said, "This is too messed up, Henry."

Henry pondered that for a few moments, and then they all left.

Alex shook Maura awake and helped her to get dressed. He saw her pendant on the floor and slipped it into the front pocket of her jeans. She was having trouble walking, so he guided her downstairs and then to his car.

A little later, after she had puked a few times, they were parked outside a Dunkin' Donuts. Alex went in and bought her a muffin and a large black coffee. He kept asking if she was okay, but she wouldn't answer. Finally he gave up and drove her home, pulling into her driveway a few minutes before midnight, just as he had promised.

He was relieved, but also a bit rattled. He thought he had figured out Maura's personality—what she was capable of—but now he wasn't so sure.

* * *

11

Maura had never been drunk before. But she liked these rum and Cokes. She knew she was high but wasn't concerned. If anything, she felt more like herself. She even considered slipping into her bathing suit. She wandered around the pool, laughing at silly jokes and flirting with a few guys, feeling comfortable enough to poke fun at Alex's reputation as a gunslinger. That wasn't nice, but what an insanely stupid nickname.

Still, she didn't want to get Alex mad. Every girl at school knew he was hot, and he'd been nice to her, so she had no problem trailing him to the greenhouse. They started to make out, though this time it was different. He seemed angry and pushed her against a glass wall. That scared her, so she fought back, but then Alex became the gentle and considerate Alex she thought she knew, so she gave in, even agreeing to follow him to the main house. She finished her fifth rum and Coke on the way, and that's when the real buzz arrived. The poolside splashing and laughter became amplified, and the harsh floodlights made her see spots.

Disoriented, she started to wobble. When she almost fell, Alex squeezed her hand and led her toward Henry's air-conditioned house, then upstairs to a bedroom. It had to be a girl's bedroom because of the soft pink comforter and pink pillows that covered the bed. On the dresser were what looked like old music boxes. She was about to examine one when Alex pushed her onto the bed.

"No," she said. "I'm really out of it."

"So am I," he said, but that didn't stop him. She felt the weight of his chest on hers, and then he started to kiss her, but something didn't seem right. She became woozy again and very, very tired. Who falls asleep when they're kissing someone? she thought.

"I want to go home," she said.

But he ignored her, trying to unbutton her blouse and unzip her jeans.

She pushed him away, but he kept at it. "No," she said, as loudly as she could.

"Geez, Maura, calm down," Alex said.

She should've kept yelling, but the five rum and Cokes had deadened her reflexes. When she tried to escape from underneath him, he ignored her, and that's when her whole body seemed to go numb.

All she could say was, "Please don't, Alex." She repeated it a number of times, but he was too strong. She had always wondered about sex, never imagining it would be so rough or take so long.

After he was done, she pretended to be asleep, even when the other boys came in, followed by the clicks of cellphone cameras. Her next clear recollections were of throwing up into some bushes beside Alex's car, then finding herself in a Dunkin' Donuts parking lot, where Alex wouldn't stop talking. He made fun of some girl who had taken her top off and jumped into the pool; he said he didn't even know Henry's friends; he asked if she wanted another muffin. He didn't look at her as he rambled on. She wanted to jump out of the car and run home, but she was in no condition to do that. Finally, at her house, he said, "Do you want me to walk you to the door?"

Do you want me to walk you to the door? Do you want me to walk you to the door? Was he serious?

After that night, he seemed to avoid her in the halls, and she waited one whole week for him to call and answer the question she'd been obsessed with, the one that jolted her from sleep every night: Why?

She knew of course what she was supposed to do: confide in her mother or a school counselor or call the police. But Alex was popular and his father was rich. He'd say they were both drunk, and everyone would ask why she'd waited so long to report it. She had seen on TV how women were treated when they came forward.

So all she was left with was confusion.

And anger.

* * *

Alex wasn't going to tell Campbell or his other friends about the party but they always expected a report, so he gave enough details to make them go away. He was aware something had gone wrong that night, and he needed to move on.

It was 9 p.m., still about seventy degrees—a nice night to take a run along the bicycle path that circled Echo Pond. That's what he'd been doing since the weather had warmed up. He had even jogged there with

13

Maura once, then made out with her in the woods nearby.

He was in front of his house, stretching out his back and hamstrings on the sidewalk, about to step into the street, when an old minivan rushed by, almost hitting him. He shook his fist and swore at the driver, but then gathered himself and jogged toward the path. Halfway through his run, he stopped at a water fountain and drank deeply. When he looked up, Maura was about thirty feet away, sitting on a large boulder that kids fished from during the day.

Faint light from a nearby lamppost made it possible to see her face, which was expressionless. She wore jeans, running shoes, and a white hoodie with the school's insignia on it. She was facing him, her hands concealed in the pockets of the hoodie. He was surprised at how little she meant to him. Looking at her was like hearing an old song and not remembering why he had ever liked it. He thought about ignoring her and sprinting away, but he was curious.

"I'm guessing this isn't a coincidence," he said.

"No, it isn't," she responded.

He placed his hands on his hips and took a deep breath. "I was going to call."

"No, you weren't."

She was right about that. "Look, Maura, school's over in a few weeks, so let's be civil and remember the good times."

A second later, he was sorry he'd said that. It was a line that had worked before, but he needed something special for Maura. He should have been patient. He should have sized her up, guessed at her intentions, then worked that angle. But it was too late now, so he decided to get tough.

"Look," he said. "I've tried to be nice, but if you don't stop stalking me, I'm going to get a restraining order. You know my father can make that happen."

That's when she showed him the gun.

* * *

Maura knew about Alex's nightly runs and his routine stop by the water fountain, so she wasn't surprised when he appeared on the sidewalk in running shorts and a T-shirt. But she wasn't prepared for what happened next. As he was stretching with his back to her, she started the minivan and in a moment of rage sped by, nearly grazing him.

Scared, she turned down the first side street she saw, where she shut down the engine and tried to calm down.

She was glad she hadn't hit him. She didn't want to make him a victim and ruin her plan. It was better to scare him. No one would believe that she had threatened to shoot him on the bike path, of all places, and if he told anyone, she'd already chosen a place to bury the gun. She would just laugh and act like he was crazy.

After regaining her composure, she drove to an empty parking lot by the path and walked toward a large boulder near the pond, not far from the fountain. That's where she waited, feeling the weight of the gun in the pocket of her hoodie.

She wasn't surprised when he approached, or when he spoke casually to her, as if he were still in control. *The Gunslinger,* she thought, a rush of anger seizing her.

But there was also something pathetic about him. He was so clueless that, for a moment, she almost ditched her plan. But how could she forget that night, how long he had kept at it, how often she had protested? How could she forget walking the gauntlet of his friends as they leaned against their lockers, smirking at her, or how the huge banners decorating the walls and congratulating the "Class of 2018" seemed, with their optimism, to mock her? And then he had to make that comment about the "good times," as if she were a little girl who could be bought off with a happy memory. She had no choice but to wave the gun in his face.

* * *

"Whoa," he said. "Is this a joke?"

It must be a toy gun, he thought.

But upon reaching her, he realized the gun was real. He thought about running but then remembered that this was Maura holding the gun, and he knew the kind of girl she was. She had confided her fears and insecurities to him. She had trusted him. She didn't have the guts to shoot anyone, he thought. She was just trying to frighten him. Yeah—that had to be it.

He moved closer to her. "No need to wave that gun if you want an apology, Maura," he said, trying to sound as calm as possible.

"I want you to kneel," she said.

He decided to go with his hunch. "I won't do that, Maura. I'm leaving, so you might as well put the gun away."

"I wouldn't do that if I were you," she said.

But he turned anyway and started toward the bike path. That's when he heard it: a metallic click.

At first he had trouble catching his breath, but then he realized the gun was indeed empty and that his hunch was right. Maura was angry, but she wasn't crazy.

So he kept walking, imagining what a gunshot might actually sound like.

Two more empty clicks broke the silence.

He smiled.

Would it be like fireworks, he thought, a hammer hitting a board a few inches from his ear, the crash of a boulder dropped from an extreme height?

He moved farther away, confident that he would never hear one of those sounds.

But then he did.

MUSCLE

At the sound of the bang, Robert nearly fell off the edge of his bed.

He'd been teaching himself Latin when he nodded off to *amo, amas, amat* echoing in his ears. The discipline of conjugating Latin verbs would've been torture for most kids, but to Robert the letters and words sang as sweetly as any backyard bird, each utterance a tiny door leading him to a past world so different from his own.

From his bedroom window he could see in the distance the calm flatness of Echo Pond. The noise seemed to come from there. Probably someone clumsily loading a boat onto a trailer after a late night of fishing.

But then again maybe the bang was a dream sound. It wasn't unlike Robert to be chased or shot at in nightmares, though at that moment he couldn't remember what images had filled his head only minutes before.

Besides Latin verbs, Robert was thinking about his name. How formal it was. Kids had tried to call him Bob, or Bobby, or Rob, but his mother made sure the Robert stuck. It was her father's name, and, as she never failed to mention, "No one ever called *him* Bob. Nicknames are for pets."

He wondered if a name actually changed a person. He pictured a kid named Rob, fifteen pounds lighter than him, running track or sinking a three-pointer to win the big game, a kid with a flat stomach who Dory Scheff and her crew would admire as he swaggered past their lockers. He wondered if you could be that kind of guy and still be interesting, because, in spite of his looks, Robert knew he was interesting.

"There are two kinds of people in this world," his mother once said, "those who read and those who don't read," and Robert had certainly read. He had devoured novels by authors other kids hated. He had read biographies, mythology, sports books, science books, even a book on the invention of dirigibles.

Could you be this imaginary Rob and still be able to carry on intelligent conversations with other interesting people? One thing for sure, no one could ever say Robert didn't have interesting friends. There was Marty Scanlon, who knew more about film than Spike Lee; Marty's girlfriend, Lucille Gorski, who'd read even more than Robert; and X-Ray, a black kid who spoke like a poet and was so far out on the fringe he sometimes spooked people.

But of all of Robert's friends, Rishi Patil and Barney Roth were the ones he found most interesting.

Barney Roth. No chance of being cool with that name. But Barney and Rishi and the others got along, so much so that since sixth grade, they were banished (happily, from their point of view) to their own lunch table because no one knew what to make of them. A kid might ask Barney, "What's up?" and he was more than capable of quoting a price from the Stock Exchange. Or if he was in a real bad mood and wanted to bust someone, he'd say, "What's up? The Carbon Index, because of that gas-guzzling Land Rover your dad just bought," or "What's up? The ticket price to *La Traviata*," which would make kids run off to the Internet to see if they'd been insulted.

It was one thing to be smart, but another to be so smart that only two or three other people knew what you were talking about, so that your jokes either went totally unnoticed or appeared to be insults that seriously annoyed people.

And that's what happened to Robert about three weeks before that bang jolted him from his nap. It started when he ran into Campbell McVeigh one night outside of the hardware store where he'd gone to buy plastic for a miniature hovercraft he was building. Campbell usually looked like that good-looking, confident Rob who Robert imagined himself being, though, at that moment, he was sitting unhappily on a curb. He tried to smile at Robert, but nothing could hide the fact that he was having a bad night: not his wavy blond hair, perfectly clipped an inch above his collar; not his electric blue eyes; and not those annoyingly adorable dimples God had blessed him with.

So Robert was stunned when Campbell said, "What's up, Hammersmith?"

Robert thought about saying, "The Carbon Index," but he was more politic than Barney, not to mention it would be bush league to steal Barney's material.

Campbell smiled again, those two dimples sinking deeper into his cheeks. "I said, What's up?"

"Just buying a few sheets of plastic," Robert said.

"Plastic?"

"Yeah, for a hovercraft."

Campbell started to laugh.

"A miniature hovercraft."

"I wish that's all I had to think about," Campbell said.

All he had to think about? Did he have any idea how hard it was to make a hovercraft?

"Yeah," was all Robert could counter with.

Campbell stood, then slowly raised his hands over his head, as if stretching. He was a foot taller than Robert. "Would you mind walking with me, Maurice?" he said.

"My name's Robert."

"Sorry, I thought it was Maurice. I'm probably thinking about your friend, the tall Pakistani dude who's always in the Science Olympiad."

"His name's Rishi, and he's Indian."

"Well, I know there's some ridiculously smart kid named Maurice somewhere."

"That would probably be a safe bet."

Campbell looked startled, and then pissed off. He could be unpredictable and spooky like that. He rarely blinked, as if wires were crossed and constantly misfiring in his head. Robert had also heard that his family was into guns. "You making fun of me?" Campbell said.

That certainly wouldn't be hard, Robert thought, but he decided not to be *too* smart that night. His mother always said it was important for "people like us" to "reach out" to people like Campbell, "not to kiss their behinds, mind you," but "to let them know we Hammersmiths can carry our own weight."

So Robert decided to do some reaching out. "No, I wasn't making fun of you. I guess I'm just distracted."

That response seemed to relax Campbell. "Well then, Maurice, would you mind walking with me?"

"It's Robert."

Campbell rested a hand on Robert's shoulder. "Sorry, it won't happen again. I'm on my way to Rite Aid, and I have a problem you might be able to solve."

A problem? Robert thought. What kind of problem does a kid like Campbell McVeigh have? Jock itch? A pair of lost Wayfarers?

"There's this girl," Campbell said, "and, well, you know how it goes. One thing, then the next, and it looks like I'll need some condoms. The problem is, the pharmacist is my mother's friend and the condoms are right under her nose."

"Why don't you go to the Rite Aid in Riverside?" Robert suggested.

"No, that's too far and I have to meet this girl right now," Campbell said, winking. "Get my drift?"

Although Robert did, indeed, get Campbell's drift, he knew absolutely nothing about condoms.

"So," Campbell said, "when I saw you going into the hardware store, I thought, 'Now there's a smart dude who might be able to help.'"

Robert kept placing one foot after the other, walking mindlessly with Campbell. "Being smart doesn't have anything to do with buying condoms," he said.

"For some reason, Robert, I have a feeling you won't have a problem."

Robert knew exactly what accounted for that feeling. He knew that Campbell knew that when the cashier took one look at Robert, this short, slightly overweight kid with freckles and longish curly black hair, she'd think he was buying the condoms for someone else, maybe his older brother.

"You think you could do this for me, Robert?" Campbell asked. "I'll make it up to you. Promise." He spoke almost in a whisper, as if he and

Robert were partners in some grand conspiracy.

Robert's first reaction was to tell Campbell to go to hell, but he was intrigued by the idea of being on an adventure with a guy like Campbell. He often thought the cool kids would like him if they ever took the time, and here was his chance. No doubt Campbell would tell everyone how Robert helped him to get laid. But Robert wanted more than that.

"Who's the girl?" he asked.

Campbell's head snapped back. "Ah, come on, I can't tell you that."

"No name, no condoms," Robert said, enjoying his advantage.

Campbell's eyes narrowed as he sized up Robert. "So you're a tough little guy, huh?"

Hey, why not? Robert thought, smiling.

Campbell hesitated, then said, "Dory Scheff."

Robert tried to look unaffected, but he couldn't stop his heart from plunging somewhere in the general vicinity of his large intestines. Since sophomore year, Dory's face had been the one he had mentally transplanted onto his fantasy girls. This put him in a strange position. How could he buy the condoms, then go home and sleep soundly with the image of a dummy like Campbell mounting the main object of his desire?

So he was surprised to find himself five minutes later clutching the twenty-dollar bill Campbell had given him and staring at dozens of brands of condoms dangling from a row of metal hooks. It was more disorienting than navigating the cereal aisle in the grocery store. So many brands and no way to know the best one. There were latex condoms, others made from polyisoprene (whatever that was). There were condoms that sped up or slowed down ejaculation. There was one brand with a "reservoir tip and a silky smooth and long-lasting lubricant," and another one you could put on with one hand. There were regular, large, and extra-large condoms, and even one that gave you a coupon for a vibrator.

Faced with such mind-boggling variety, Robert was almost (*almost*) glad he was still a virgin. But he was also angry he'd put himself in this situation. To make matters worse, Heather James, a classmate and an acolyte at his church, was working the cash register. He knew he couldn't look into those God-fearing blue eyes and ask her to ring up a package of Durex Avanti Bare Latex Condoms. But most of all he was mad at Campbell, who was probably sitting on a promotional lawn chair outside the sliding glass doors laughing his ass off.

And that's when he got his idea to steal a box of the largest condoms available. It was a black box with NINJA printed boldly in gold on the outside. Under the NINJA, in smaller type, was BE A WARRIOR, and under that, EXTRA EXTRA LARGE AND LONG CONDOMS. He thought Campbell would like the warrior part, but with his huge ego he'd never consider whether the condoms would be too big.

Although Robert had never stolen anything before, a different Robert (maybe that Rob with the flat stomach) was in charge now, so he scanned the store to see if he was being watched before sliding the box into his pocket. Once it was hidden, he opened it with one hand, took out the three attached packets, then hid the empty box next to a display of protein bars. He bought a bar on his way out and even chatted with Heather James about church school.

Outside, he handed the condoms to Campbell.

"Ninja," Campbell said, looking at the packet. Then, "Warrior. I like that." Followed by, "Why aren't they in a box?"

"I stole them," Robert said.

Campbell looked around as if expecting the condom police to show up. "That took balls, Maurice."

Robert sure didn't feel ballsy. In fact, he felt just the opposite, as if he had somehow betrayed all the interesting, unattractive people all over the world, particularly those kids who had ever been called geeks or losers, the ones who sat home on Saturday nights watching old *Twilight Zone* episodes while the cool kids smoked dope and got laid.

"Yeah, Maurice," Campbell said. "Real balls." Then he thanked Robert before walking away.

"It's Robert," Robert said, but Campbell wasn't listening.

A few days later Robert was hanging out after school by the bike rack with Barney and Rishi. Barney was describing an old *X-Files* episode about an archangel who was sent to bring girls he'd fathered back to heaven. "He had to fry them with heavenly light before taking their souls," Barney said. "Now that's the kind of God I could believe in."

"I remember that episode," Rishi said. "But it wasn't based on the Bible. It was from a story even the Church thinks is bogus."

"You mean in contrast to the fact-based Garden of Eden with the talking snake?"

"It was about love," Robert said.

"What was?" Barney said.

"That episode. The angel loved the girls. He wanted to put them out of their pain."

"So he fried them? I mean, there was smoke coming out of their eyes."

The three of them would have argued all afternoon if they hadn't been interrupted by the tennis team heading for the courts, led by Campbell McVeigh. Robert had seen him a few times since he'd bought the condoms. He had expected him to say hi or at least to pat him on the back, but it seemed Robert's plan had worked too well and Campbell had figured it out. Robert had told Barney and Rishi about the Extra Extra Large and Long Condoms and had sworn them to secrecy, which was driving Barney nuts.

But all that was about to change.

At first, Campbell looked like he might pass harmlessly by, but then he veered off, stopping a few feet away.

"You guys having a good time?"

Rishi and Barney weren't used to being talked to by kids like Campbell unless they were being insulted, so even Barney was speechless for a second.

"You knew about the condoms, didn't you?" Campbell said.

"The condoms?" Robert said.

Campbell pointed his racket at Robert. "You know what I'm talking about, Maurice."

Robert continued to play dumb, and for a second he thought he might pull it off, but then Barney had to get cute. "His name's Robert."

"Maurice. Robert. What does it matter? You guys are almost invisible anyway."

"You mean like your penis?" Barney said.

"Cool it, Barney," Robert said.

"You told these geeks?" Campbell said. "Anyone else know?"

"Relax, Campbell," Robert said. "I think there's been a misunderstanding."

"More like a mismeasurement," Barney said. "Dude, do you know the penis you have at eighteen is the one you're stuck with for the rest of your life?"

"Now you're in real fucking trouble, Maurice," Campbell said.

"What's with this guy?" Barney said. "He's got the short-term memory of a squirrel."

Robert almost laughed at that one, but the demented look on Campbell's face stifled that impulse.

As Campbell continued to glare at him, gripping his racket, Robert wondered if anyone had ever been murdered with such a weapon.

"Fuck all of you dinks," Campbell said before trotting off toward the tennis courts.

Barney was about to offer a wisecrack, probably on the word *dink*, when Robert said, "Shut up, Barney. You just made everything worse."

"You mean you won't be going to the prom with him? What's up, Robert? That fuckhead can't even get your name right. Why do you care what he thinks?"

"Barney's got a point," Rishi said.

"Oh, fuck you, Reesh," Robert said.

"Totally unnecessary," Rishi said.

Which got them all sniping at each other until they went their separate ways.

The next week was torture for Robert. Every time Campbell or one of his friends passed him in the hall, they'd bump him hard, trying to knock off his backpack. One time, Campbell, pretending to be helpful, picked up the backpack but then swung it into Robert's balls. Robert went to his knees while a group of jocks laughed loudly. For the rest of the day he found himself involuntarily twitching as he moved from class to class, wondering when the next attack would occur. He knew it was just a matter of time until Campbell got him alone and beat the hell out of him.

"We have to do something," Barney said one day when he and Robert were sitting on a boat launch at Echo Pond, throwing tiny stones into the water.

"We?"

"Hey, it was my fault."

"You're evolving, Barney. It only took two weeks to admit that."

"Sorry, but I couldn't stand listening to that asshole."

"Whatever, dude. I think I'm going to have to ride it out until school ends."

"No, that's too long. It's time for Muscle."

Robert laughed. "You don't really think that exists, do you? That'd make you as dumb as Campbell."

All of senior year there was a rumor that some badass guys had started a club called Muscle, and for a price they'd intimidate someone or even smack them around if necessary. Everyone knew that one of those guys had to be Adam Igoe, but who'd ever publicly say that unless they wanted to get punched out.

"I've done some checking," Barney said, rubbing his hands together, very pleased with himself.

"You don't let up, do you?"

"Just talk to Igoe. I told him you'd meet him at nine under that gazebo by the kids' park."

"Should I wear a disguise?"

"It's up to you."

Robert shook his head. "I was joking, Barney. What did you tell him?"

"Just general stuff."

"And what did he say?"

"He said he'd been waiting a long time to hear from one of us. What do you think he meant by that?"

"You're kidding, right?"

"I'm actually not."

"He meant that we're the kind of guys who get made fun of a lot."

"Well, I don't see that," Barney said.

"Yeah, you probably don't."

Barney stood and threw a handful of dirt and stones into the woods behind him. "Whatever, Maurice, it's your call. Do you want to be in therapy the rest of your life, flinching every time you walk by some kid at college, or do you want to strike back?"

And so Robert found himself under the gazebo shortly after nightfall, arranging to pay Adam Igoe twenty dollars down to intimidate Campbell McVeigh, then twenty dollars a few weeks later if Robert was satisfied. Much to Robert's surprise, the first payment was worth it, since Campbell had stopped hassling him. That's why he was glad that loud bang had jolted him awake. He owed Adam the remaining twenty dollars that night, and he didn't want to keep him waiting.

For early June it was hot. By the time Robert reached the gazebo, the moon, almost full, had risen, a few stars taking their expected places in the sky. Adam was late, so Robert hoped he hadn't messed up on the time. Normally, by 9 p.m. Robert's town was as dead as Lindsay Lohan's career, but red flashing lights and the wail of sirens filled the night. Cop cars went rushing by, and for a moment Robert thought they might be coming for him. Three weeks ago, who would've thought he'd end up stealing condoms and hiring a hit man?

Fortunately, the lights and wails disappeared down Spruce Street in the direction of Echo Pond. Before Robert could guess the reason for this unusual activity, he saw a figure in a white T-shirt exiting a wooded path behind him and walking slowly toward the gazebo.

It was Adam.

Adam wasn't a tall dude, but he was solid. Barney called him The Hulk because he was so muscled that his arms and legs looked like thick intertwined ropes covered with a thin layer of skin. His head resembled a stripped skull—a chiseled appearance that was exaggerated by his shaved head. He had a strange habit of pursing his lips when annoyed, as he was now. "You didn't call them, did you?" Adam said, in a voice as hoarse and menacing as a garbage disposal.

"Who?" Robert asked.

"The cops."

"If I had, they wouldn't have driven away."

"You making fun of me?"

In fact, Robert wasn't. "I'd never do that, dude," he said.

Adam pursed his lips again. "I told you the last time not to call me dude. You stupid wangstas make me sick." He pointed to the bench on the gazebo and gestured for Robert to sit down. "Welcome to my office."

"What?"

"It was a joke, jerk-off."

If Adam thought it was a joke, then that was good enough for Robert, so he laughed and sat down. He was surprised when Adam joined him. Adam rested his arm on top of the backrest behind Robert, so that Robert could see the dark hairs sprouting from his armpit. Noticing that Robert's eyes were fixated there, Adam lowered his arm and placed his hands onto his lap, interlocking his fingers and sliding them slowly back and forth. "Campbell bothering you anymore?" he asked.

"No."

"So do you have the rest of the money?"

Robert handed Adam some bills, which Adam stuffed into his back pocket.

"I want you to know I don't have anything against you," Adam said.

"Yeah, you made that clear before."

"I mean, you don't piss me off or anything."

"Good."

"Before I go, I need to show you something."

"What?"

"Just follow me, okay?"

Robert shadowed Adam as he climbed down the gazebo and headed toward a path in the woods.

"Where're we going?" Robert said.

"Just a little farther," Adam said, leading Robert a few paces into the woods.

When they stopped, Adam said, "Nothing personal," and he punched Robert in the face.

Robert lay on the ground, too afraid to stand.

"You can get up," Adam said. "I'm not going to hit you again."

Robert stood and rubbed the area below his cheekbone.

"I made sure I didn't hit you square in the eye or nose," Adam said, proud of his expertise.

"Why did you hit me at all?" Robert asked.

"Because Campbell paid me fifty bucks to do it."

"But I paid you, too."

Adam nodded. "Yeah, and I did what you wanted, right?"

"Does that mean we're all square now?"

"Why? Are you going to the cops?"

That option had crossed Robert's mind. "No," he said.

"Why not?"

"Why do you care?"

Adam seemed offended. "I may seem like a dumb shit, but I've always wondered why people do things."

"Like punching someone in the face?"

"No, I know why I did that."

"If I don't say why I'm not calling the cops," Robert said, "are you going to hit me again?"

"No. Like I said, I like you better than Campbell. For another twenty-five bucks, I'll kick his ass for you."

"Only twenty-five?"

"Like I said, you've never done anything shitty to me. He has."

"I'm not telling anyone, Adam," Robert said, "because I'm afraid of you, and because I probably deserved to get punched for messing around with an asshole like Campbell."

"Still, tell me if he hassles you. He knows I'm watching him."

"I guess I'm supposed to say thanks."

"You trying to be funny again?"

Robert rubbed the welt beginning to rise from his cheek. "I'm not feeling very funny right now."

"Just one more thing," Adam said.

Robert was waiting for Adam to pull out a knife and stab him a few times. What was the going rate for that?

"What?" Robert asked.

"Part of the deal was that I had to say something before I left."

28

"Sure, go ahead."

"Campbell said to say, 'Fuck you, Maurice, since you'll never get the pieces of ass I've had, even if you have a dick that fits those condoms.' Remember, that's coming from him, not me."

"I appreciate that."

"I won't ask what he meant."

"I appreciate that, too."

Before Adam left, he held out his hand, and Robert shook it. "I'd put some ice on your face when you get home," he said, then turned and disappeared into the woods, apparently unafraid of any wild animals or nutcases lurking there.

To get home, Robert had to take a road that crossed Spruce Street. Up ahead he noticed flashing lights from two police cars that were parked in a lot near the bike path. He went up to a cop and asked what was going on.

"Just move along," the cop said.

Robert was about to leave when another cop ran up. "Somebody got shot."

"Shit," the other cop said, then looked at Robert. "You live far away?"

"No," Robert said.

"You want a ride home?"

"No, I'm all right."

"Okay then, but get moving."

Robert turned in the direction of his house, thinking the cops must've made a mistake. As far as he knew, no one had ever been shot in his town. Punched in the face, maybe, but not shot. As he walked away he could feel his face beginning to swell. He wanted to get home and ice it, hoping to keep the visible damage to a minimum. He didn't want his mother to drive him nuts with questions.

He wondered what Barney would say about Adam's bizarre attack, though he fancied the idea of looking like he'd been in a fight. He also knew that if Campbell hassled him again, Adam would be waiting in the wings.

And for only twenty-five dollars.

29

PRETTY GIRL

So you ask, "How could anyone so drop-dead gorgeous be afraid of mirrors?"

It's because I'm only seventeen and my face is a minefield of pimples (well, maybe only one big one) and my cheeks are this sucky red, almost like a rash. I'm starting to look like this girl named Rose Rubino, who all the boys call Rosacea because of her acne.

I was telling Megan all this when there was this mega-loud *bam* outside my bedroom window, like our metal garage door came crashing down on my dad's vintage Jaguar.

"What was that?" Megan asked.

"I think my garage door just collapsed. It's been making weird noises, but after the landscapers started eye-groping my mom, my dad said no more laborers for a while."

My mom's even prettier than me.

"Lucille," Megan said, "do you really think a garage door falling apart could be that loud? It sounded like it came from Echo Pond."

The real Lucille is this Goth girl in school, who could be pretty with a little TLC, but she hangs out with these AV guys, doing artsy-fartsy projects no one cares about. One day when we were coming out of school, she filmed us, saying, "Now here are the pretty, popular girls going to get their nails done." Trish Thurber, another one of my friends, called her a stupid bitch, and since then anytime a girl does or says anything one of us thinks is stupid we call her Lucille.

"It was probably just a gigantous tree falling," I said.

31

We live close to the country club, where a few years ago a huge tree limb broke off on the golf course and almost killed Ashley Silva's dad, which would've been a shame because he looks like that vampire dad in *Twilight*.

"You're probably right," Megan said, "but let's talk about your face. I think it's what they call facial stress."

"Facial stress?"

"Yeah, I read that your skin can get stressed out."

"You mean like have a nervous breakdown?"

"How can skin have a nervous breakdown, Lucille?"

"I don't get it," I told Megan.

"Obviously, but you can do something about it."

"Like what?"

"Go to the mirror."

And I did.

"Now look at that beautiful face, Dory. First say, 'That's the most beautiful face in the whole senior class. They might've voted Sabrina Flint homecoming queen, but no one can rock a prom like Dory Scheff.'"

Which happens to be true, though I think my prom dress was what really destroyed them. My mother had wanted me to wear this classic satiny thing that made me look like Jane Eyre, but I talked her into a Drew Jacquard two-piece dress that caught everyone off-guard.

Even Megan doesn't have the abs to wear that dress.

"But what about this big pimple on my forehead?" I said. "I look like a Cyclops, and my eyes are so saggy you'd think they're having babies."

"Please, no more about the eyes, you bitch."

We both laughed because that's the way we talk to each other. Some people think we're airheads, but they're just haters, like Lucille. Megan and I both got into good colleges. That didn't happen because we're stupid. And who plans on working after college, anyway? Isn't the point to meet a guy?

"Now about your eyes, Dory," Megan said. "I've been doing some reading. It's like you got all these blood vessels overlapping like spider webs, and when you're stressed, they expand or explode, I forget which."

"Gross."

"So, first, you need more sleep, and then—wait a minute, I wrote it down—you gotta 'hydrate and exfoliate,' and use a 'lightweight face oil with salicylic acid.' After school we can go to Melanctha's. That's where my mom buys her stuff."

My mom says Megan's mom tries too hard to be pretty. That must be tough.

"But I get enough sleep," I said.

"I'm talking about *good* sleep. You're always obsessing, and remember, every time you obsess, more and more blood vessels explode."

"Omigod," I said, wanting to ask more questions, but that's when an annoying scream of sirens broke the silence. By the time I reached my window the noise had stopped, replaced by bright red flashing lights that made the copper weathervane on top of my garage glow. I told Megan about it and she said I should check it out.

"No way," I said.

"Why not? You could end up on TV."

"With my luck, some guy will be dead, and instead of filming that, the cameraman will zero in on my Cyclops pimple. Then a reporter will ask, 'Young lady, did you know the deceased?' and I'll say, 'Yes, it was Mr. Gladstone. By all accounts he was an ace golfer and first-class pervert who eye-groped me every morning when I jogged by his house. It makes sense that he'd strangle his golden Lab, then turn a gun on himself.'"

We both laughed, but as it turned out, it wasn't very funny. The next day at school we learned that someone had shot Alex Youngblood. I mean, he was dead. I felt so very weird, like I was a part of it. Just two weeks ago at Luke Kelly's party Alex got drunk and groped me under this gorgeous Japanese maple tree. I pushed him away, but if I hadn't, we might've been a thing for a while, like he was my boyfriend, and everyone would've been asking me how I felt about him getting shot.

Right before first period, I was explaining this to Megan and to another friend of ours, Jamie, and Megan said, "You really *are* a narcissistic bitch."

Megan and I started poking each other, but Jamie didn't laugh, which wasn't a surprise. Her boyfriend was killed in a car accident a few months ago, and overnight Jamie became Zombie Jamie, though she had started distancing herself from us as soon as the boy came on the scene. He was an InstaStalker and a Mr. Question Guy, all over Jamie like perfume, so we thought she'd stop being Stepford Wife Jamie after he died. But instead, gasp, she became Zombie Jamie and then Gandhi Jamie, sharing all these supposedly profound ideas on everything, like she was better than us. She said, and I'm quoting, "Proximity to death has made me more loving of others." I mean, we all say stuff like that in church school and on college essay applications, but I know for a fact that Jamie got knocked out during the accident. How can you have "proximity" to something you don't remember?

Hashtag: girl drama.

After first period, the day got even weirder. It seemed like every five minutes we were told that counselors were available in the auditorium if we felt depressed, though no one was rushing off to see them. Alex wasn't the kind of boy you'd miss. I mean, he never paid much attention to anyone but himself. But I still wanted to find out who killed him, and I was disappointed when the police didn't question me.

By the time school ended, I was more tired of Alex than when he was alive, so I wasn't very happy when my mother started in about it. We were sitting on the patio sipping iced tea. She wanted to know what the school said ("Dunno!"), if the police had any clues ("Dunno!"), and if I was afraid to go out at night now ("Really?").

"So you're saying, young lady, that you have no feelings about the shooting of a boy you grew up with?"

"I just don't have any feelings about it *right now*," I said. "Maybe I'll be sad later. I heard that can happen."

I didn't believe that, but my mother's been in therapy since she was born, so I knew what she wanted to hear. I often wonder what she complains about to her shrink. How she got a varicose vein after my brother was born? How her Pilates instructor had an attack of appendicitis and was replaced by this really obnoxious Latino woman named Magdalena?

"Well, I'm here for you, Dory. Do you hear what I'm saying?"

"Well, yeah, I'm right next to you. How can I *not* hear?"

She shook her head. Sometimes she reminds me of Jamie, like she's totally baffled or frustrated by what I say. Maybe there's a Jamie virus going around turning everyone into do-gooders or what Megan calls "feelies," people who love misery more than Botox.

But my mother wasn't done yet. "I'm trying to decide whether I should call Alex's mother."

"You're what?"

"Well, I'm on three committees with her. She's a nice woman, and we planned to push you and Alex into driving the Mobile Cloak van this summer."

She was referring to this van our church sends out every week that's loaded with clothes for the homeless. I tried to picture Alex and me handing out clothes in the kind of neighborhood we've only seen on *CSI* episodes. I believe it's important to know who you are, and driving the Mobile Cloak van isn't Dory Scheff.

"Why don't *you* do it with me?" I said.

You should have seen the panic on her face. "Because that's not my job. I just organize the trips."

Yeah, because you don't want to do the dirty work, I felt like saying. You don't want to fold or pack the clothes or talk to a bunch of smelly people with no teeth. I'd like to lay that truth bomb on her, but I'll probably be doing the same thing in fifteen years. That's what all her friends do, just so they can hold charity balls and see themselves in *Rhode Island Monthly*.

"I don't mind bringing in canned goods," I said. "I don't mind the Secret Santa stuff, either, though I can't see some poor girl from South Providence walking around with an Ocher Dior bracelet without getting mugged. But I already did what you forced me to so I'd get into a good college."

"That's not why our family does community service," she said.

"The only community service Dad does is tipping his caddie."

I could tell she was angry because she kept moving her glass around on the patio table, which made an annoying screeching sound.

"From the day I started high school," I reminded her, "you said I needed to get 'credentials' for a 'premier' college. Play a sport, join a few clubs, and do community service so people thought I had a social conscience."

"I don't think those were my exact words," she said.

I was going to call her on that, but fortunately she was done quizzing me, so I didn't have to think about Alex again until an hour later when Megan called to say there was going to be a vigil.

"Who put that together?" I asked.

"Missy Rogers."

"Give me a Xanax. She barely knew Alex."

I could hear Megan sigh. "When it comes to Missy," she said, "I gotta draw the line. When your little brother dies of cancer, you get a pass on any crazy thing you feel like doing."

Missy's ten-year-old brother died about a year ago from a weird form of blood cancer. Since then, we've rarely seen her mother, and her younger brother, who's a sophomore, keeps getting into trouble. But I usually keep my mouth shut about that, because Missy's father is my dad's boss at the bank.

"I just can't stand that do-gooder saint stuff anymore," I said.

That's what some of the kids call Missy. The Saint.

"Well, do you think we should go?" Megan asked.

"I don't have a choice," I said. "Alex and I were almost a thing."

"But you said you wouldn't make out with him."

"It's about intent, Lucille. Everyone knows he thought of me as a long-term thing. The least I can do is pay my respects."

"Do you know what you're going to wear?"

"What's the temperature supposed to be?"

"Very hot, maybe even eighty at night."

"I could just kill you."

"Why?"

"Because I'm totally confused now. Like, there are a bazillion possibilities."

"Whatever you do," she said, "I wouldn't attract attention to yourself. Kids will think you didn't care about Alex, and you know how a certain Lucille and her friends will have fun with that."

"Oh, screw them."

"Well, if that's how you feel, then let's pillage our closets and make a statement."

"Sounds like a plan," I said.

After I got off the phone I took Bella, our golden retriever, out to pee, then finished a final project for history class on the Vietnam War (like who cares, it was so long ago). At about ten o'clock I ended up alone in my room. It was so hot all I wore were panties and a baggy white T-shirt I bought in Cancun.

I felt depressed and lonely. I don't know if it was the heat or Alex or maybe just the headache I had from going through all my clothes. I felt somehow that it was very, very important to choose the right outfit. I'd probably never know anyone who'd get shot again. Girls like Lucille think my life is easy because I'm rich and pretty, but they can't grasp what it's like to be constantly stared at and judged. Even my dad's friends get uncomfortable around me, and more than once I've caught them staring at my ass. Gross! Being pretty, you get used to that kind of attention, but you know that if you stop looking gorgeous for two seconds, you'll vanish off the face of the earth faster than that little girl in *Poltergeist*.

When I get nervous about junk like this, I massage some jasmine vanilla oil into my temples and try to think of good things, like my prom gown or the time I set the sixth-grade record for sit-ups. When that doesn't work I reach for a tiny vial of my mother's Ativan that she thinks she's misplaced. It didn't take long for me to realize it was going to be an Ativan night, so I popped a pill. When my heart stopped its hyper beating, I closed my eyes, trying to bring back the image of my prom gown and the way everyone stared when I jogged into the auditorium, my tits bouncing like two happy pink balloons. It was like my date didn't even exist.

As it turned out I decided on a green paper-thin linen mid-length Coachella-style dress for the vigil. I really wanted to wear white short shorts and this super cute Free People silk crochet-trimmed deep V halter top, but it all seemed too daring, and Megan convinced me the boys would think I was disrespecting Alex. Personally, I think she was afraid guys would be staring at me instead of her, though I had to admit she looked great in her sheer white cotton slacks and pink strappy chiffon tank top. All those donkey kicks have paid off.

Alex's house was this huge mansion on a road that bordered the golf course but also looked out onto the bay, its back lawn only fifty yards from the beach. Megan and I arrived there right as Missy Rogers was moving from kid to kid handing out candles. If I'd been in charge I would've bought a bunch of those fluorescent sticks they use at carnivals. They're not messy and the wind can't blow them out.

Missy gave us each a candle, then lit them. She was standing so close, the flame from my candle illuminated her face, as if I was holding a giant buttercup under her chin. She stared hopefully at us, and I was reminded of how pretty she was. I had always wanted big doe eyes and puffy lips like Scarlett Johansson, and there was Missy wasting both of them on grief. I felt like hugging her, but she frightened me, like if I got too close I'd be sad too.

"Thanks for coming," was all she said, then moved to another group.

After she left, I didn't know what to say. Unfortunately, "creepy" came out, and I spent the next five minutes apologizing to Megan.

"Like I said," Megan protested, "Missy's off limits."

"Even if she's talking to that Robert geek."

And that's where she was, under a huge pine tree, chatting it up with this short, curly-haired kid named Robert Hammersmith, who was standing with his two geeky friends, Rishi Patil and Barney Something-or-Other, a kid with a really gross black unibrow, who always looks like he's about to cry and who has a stupid opinion on just about everything. Earlier in the year, he and his friends tried to start a *Dr. Who* club, which was based on a TV show older than my grandmother. When they gave me a flyer, I said, "Dr. Who?" and they all laughed. At first I was furious, but then I realized that in ten years I'd be hiring them to cut my lawn or unplug the toilet. All these smarter-than-thou haters can get by in high school, but eventually they end up owning comic book stores or working at Shaw's and talking about *Walking Dead* episodes while munching on Sugar Puffs.

Besides the *Dr. Who* crew, there were about six pockets of people you'd normally never see hanging out with each other. Kind of like those dances in eighth grade where kids pack together like scared puppies, trying to decide what they'll do if asked to dance. It was like everyone was waiting for something to happen but knowing it wouldn't because the guest of honor was dead.

But Campbell McVeigh showed up with a few jocks. I had to smile when I saw him. Just recently he had tried to devirginize me, but couldn't keep his thingy on. It wasn't going to happen anyway, but now he won't even look at me, probably because he's afraid I'll tell someone about it. It's kind of awesome having that power over a guy. He and some other jocks were sitting in a circle joking and lighting joints with their candles.

"Missy's not going to like that," I said.

"Yeah, but look who else is here," Megan said.

She was talking about Patti Rizzo.

"What's the connection there?" Megan said.

"Probably just another slut Alex hooked up with."

"Well," Megan said, "at least we know who's going to be the eye candy tonight."

I tried to stay calm, but I was fuming inside. I had spent all day picking out an outfit that would make a statement without disrespecting Alex's vigil, and then Patti shows up in a simple white, almost transparent hippie dress, separating herself from everyone else, so you have no choice but to look at her. Everyone says she's ditzy, but I don't agree. She positioned herself perfectly on the highest part of the lawn, so that the breeze off the bay blew her long, curly blond hair behind her like she was posing for a *Vanity Fair* photo shoot. To make it worse, the house's floodlights struck her from behind, making her glow like that exotic Elf queen in *The Hobbit*.

I stood there for a moment, taking in the scene, while the jocks continued to act up. Everything seemed a teeny bit surreal, like maybe the breeze had blown a marijuana cloud our way. It was then that my worst nightmare bumped into me: Lucille Gorski (what kind of last name is that?) and her boyfriend, Marty Scanlon. They were lugging their cameras, obviously intending to film parts of the vigil.

"I'm outta here," I said to Megan.

39

We blew out our candles, hoping that might make our exit invisible, but Lucille wasn't going to let that happen.

"And what brings the popular girls here tonight?" she said, holding the camera a few feet from my face.

"It's not even on," I said.

"Omigod," she said. "Like, you're totally right. What a mega mistake. I shoulda stayed home and painted my nails or mega obsessed about the color panties I was going to wear tomorrow."

"We don't talk like that," Megan said.

Marty Scanlon laughed, then said, "Let it go, Lucille."

"Totally, Marty. No problemo."

They started to walk away, but I was mad now. I thought of everything I went through to be there, only to get insulted by a dwarf with short uncombed brown hair, who was wearing black Levi's, a white T-shirt, and black Converse basketball sneakers. (Can anyone say "Ellen DeGeneres"?)

"You know what you are?" I said to her.

She turned, and it was clear she was interested. "No, what am I, Cinderella?"

It was one of those big moments in life, but I couldn't think of anything to say.

"Come on, Lucille, let it go," Marty said.

"No, I want to know what Cinderella thinks of me."

A ton of ideas fluttered through my mind, but what popped out was, "You're a Lucille, that's what you are."

Marty and Lucille seemed baffled by my comment, but Megan knew what I meant. "Yeah," she said, "you're so, so Lucille."

And that got us both laughing until we noticed that kids were looking at us like we were crazy, so we decided we'd had enough of mourning and left.

Half an hour later I found myself alone in my room, still unable to shake the image of Patti getting all that attention without even trying to be pretty. Frustrated, I went over to the mirror and began to work on my pimple. As I cleansed and scrubbed it, I kept thinking about the vigil, angry that I'd gone. Life's weird. You try to do something nice but end up realizing why it's best to stay away from death and sadness and people who will probably struggle their whole lives just to buy a nice car. I know how bad that sounds, but you can't save the world, and haters can bring you down faster than a zombie virus.

After I cleaned the area around the pimple I rubbed in the oil Megan and I had bought at Melanctha's. It really worked, and I made Megan promise not to tell anyone else about it. I know that's sucky, but beauty is partly about secrets, and you can always share them later, maybe in ten years when we'll all have crow's-feet and toenail fungus, and be married with kids, and our lives, gasp, will be basically over.

GRAVEYARD LOVE

Marty Scanlon knew from the get-go it was a gunshot. He had watched enough Tarantino movies and made so many of his own that he could even guess the make of the gun, a Ruger SP101 Standard. Marty had heard the sounds of guns exploding in a cave, inside a small room, and outside in the open. He had scoured every free sound-effects site on the Internet at one time or another. This gunshot was definitely outside in the open, slightly muffled, probably by surrounding trees.

So he wasn't surprised the next day when he learned that Alex Youngblood had taken a bullet through the heart while out running on the bike path. No one would ever admit to it, but there was a long line of kids who would've pulled that trigger.

"So why am I looking at a bunch of stoned jocks chasing each other around with candles?" Barney Roth said.

Barney, one of Marty's friends, was in Marty's basement about five days after the shooting, staring at a huge flat-screen TV, along with Rishi Patil and Lucille Gorski, Marty's girlfriend.

"You're looking in the wrong place," Marty said.

"I don't see anything, either," Lucille said. "What about you, Reesh?"

"Nada," Rishi said.

"They're right there," Marty said. He pointed to an area near the woods. "Right there."

"That foggy spot?" Rishi said.

"Well, what about the porch? Look on the porch."

"More fog?"

"Ah, I see where we're going now," Barney said. "This is your ghost shit, right?"

"Oh, Marty," Lucille said, looking defeated. "I thought you wanted to be taken seriously."

"I didn't go to the vigil looking for anything," Marty lied. "I was actually surprised when I played it back."

Marty was talking about the movie he'd shot on Alex Youngblood's front lawn at a vigil held two days after the murder. Although he hadn't liked Alex, he thought someone from school should record the event and give it to Alex's parents, not to mention that he had his own selfish reasons for being there.

He aimed the controller at the screen and paused the tape. "Look at those shapes by the woods, and that outline of someone on the porch."

Barney started to laugh, his black unibrow twitching like the frenzied wings of a bat.

"Don't laugh at him, Barney," Lucille said, shaking her little fist.

Marty liked it when Lucille got mad. In fact, Marty liked most everything about Lucille: the way she didn't care about what she wore (Converse basketball shoes, heavy-metal T-shirts, and black jeans); the way she walked, like she'd trounce you if you got in her way; and most important, how she believed in him. If Marty ever got around to making a real movie, he'd be picking up his Academy Award with Lucille at his side.

But he knew she'd lost patience with his ghost hunting after she'd spent one too many nights in the local cemetery, watching him experiment with different lenses, as they waited for some ghastly spirit to reveal itself.

"Leash your pit bull," Barney said, referring to Lucille. "I'm just saying I agree with Reesh about the fog thing."

Rishi looked very happy that Barney agreed with him, since, as far as Marty knew, that rarely happened.

"Maybe Marty's right," Lucille said, tracing the misty shape on the porch with her index finger.

"You saying that could be Alex?" Barney said.

"You made that connection, not me," Marty said.

"And those other shapes?"

"I'm trying to figure that out. But here's the crazy part." Marty fast-forwarded the video until he reached the image of a girl moving toward the camera. "You see it?"

"What's so crazy about Jamie Costa walking on Alex's lawn?" Barney said.

"Look at what she's doing."

"She looks like she's holding someone's hand," Lucille said, suddenly becoming interested.

"No, she's holding no one's hand," Marty said, "unless you count that hazy white blur beside her."

"That's why you wanted me and Reesh here?" Barney said. "Christ, if you look closely, you'll notice that the lights in Alex's living room are on. What you're seeing are orbs from those lights messing with your lens. That's Filmmaking 101."

"You don't know what you're talking about," Marty said. "Those shapes aren't orbs. They're apparitions, and my guess is Alex hasn't crossed over yet."

"And how does Jamie fit into this?"

"Her boyfriend was killed in that car accident a few months ago, right?"

Barney laughed again. "Jesus, what's taking him so long to make the leap?" He looked at Lucille. "You don't believe this crap, do you?"

She was staring at Jamie Costa, then backtracking to the previous scene.

"Reesh and I were at the vigil, too," Barney added, "and the only thing I saw was a bunch of stoned jocks acting like orangutans."

Rishi was sitting on a beanbag chair, squirming.

"What's your problem?" Barney said.

Rishi squirmed a little more. "You remember how Jamie was, like, talking to herself? I mean, she did it twice. You commented on it, dude."

"No, I didn't."

"Actually, you said, and I quote, 'The girl's having visions.'"

"Whose fucking side are you on?"

Rishi was a dark-skinned, lanky Indian kid, but strong. He could've easily squished Barney like the dung beetle he could sometimes be, but for some reason he usually gave in. This time, though, Barney was doing something that always drove Rishi crazy.

"First of all," Rishi said, "there are no sides. Secondly, could you lay off the swearing for about two minutes? You know how I feel about that."

"I haven't been swearing," Barney said, which made Marty and Lucille laugh. "Oh, fuck you guys. Who gets worked up about swearing, anyway?"

"I do," Rishi said. "It gets stupid after a while."

"Yeah," Lucille said. "It's a sign of insecurity, like you're saying, 'I don't think I'm cool, so if I swear a lot, you'll think I'm this real tough guy.' Also, can we stop talking about Alex like he's not a person? I mean, he could be a jerk, but we knew him, and he's dead, and it could've been us on the bike path that night."

"She's right," Marty said.

Barney's eyes widened in disbelief. "Give me a break, Lucille. You know Alex thought we were losers, and Reesh's swearing phobia has nothing to do with my insecurity. It's that Hindu shit he's into, right, Reesh?"

"I think I'm going to go," Rishi said, moving toward the stairs.

"Ah, come on, Reesh," Marty said. "Don't desert me. I need the voice of reason here. The problem is that Barney's not giving me enough credit. I went over and over this footage, and I've read enough to know the difference between an orb, a flare, and an apparition." He pointed again to the blurry shape inhabiting Alex's porch. "*This* is an apparition."

"I'm beginning to see Marty's point," Lucille said, which made Marty extraordinarily happy.

"Ah, graveyard love," Barney said. "The ecstasy of smooching beside an unmarked gravestone can really get the fucking juices flowing."

Rishi shook his head and readied himself to leave again.

"Okay, okay," Barney said. "No more swearing. But for the sake of argument, let's say those orbs are Alex and—what was the other dude's name, Jamie's dead beau?"

"Ryan Holt," Lucille said.

"Yeah, I remember now," Barney said. "He was a real douchebag."

"Ryan was okay," Lucille said.

Marty was a bit surprised by her comment. "You never told me you were friends with that dude."

"Believe it or not, I had a life before you guys," Lucille said.

Lucille could be so ornery that Marty always assumed she hadn't dated much. "Did you go out with him?"

Lucille didn't answer, but Marty could tell she was uncomfortable.

"It's not like I'd care," Marty said.

"Hello, hello," Barney said. "I thought we were talking about ghosts swarming the Youngblood residence."

Marty ignored Barney, pulling Lucille toward him and draping his arm over her shoulders. "It just seems weird you'd go out with a guy like that."

"Who cares if Lucille made out with that Ryan guy?" Barney said. "I mean, the dude's dead."

"Can't you shut up for about two seconds, Barney?" Marty said.

Frustrated by this back-and-forth, Lucille shook off Marty's arm and went back to staring at the screen.

But Marty was curious now. "Is Barney right, Lucille?"

"About what?" Lucille said, continuing to rewind and fast-forward the tape, as if she were the only person in the room.

"You know what I'm talking about."

"I gotta go," Rishi said, halfway up the basement stairs before anyone could stop him.

"Now look what you've done," Lucille said.

"That's not Marty's fault," Barney said. "Reesh has been acting weird since the shooting. Whenever I bring it up he says it was probably an accident. I mean, you don't get shot in the back by accident. The problem with Reesh is that he hasn't accepted that the world is a fucked-up place. Like I said, it's that Hindu shit."

At that moment Marty didn't care about Rishi. "Well, Lucille?"

Lucille tossed the remote onto an old, cracked black leather couch that had been pushed against a wall. "It's none of your business what happened between me and Ryan. It was like a century ago."

47

Marty wasn't so sure anymore. He'd asked a simple question. What was the big deal? And what did "what happened between me and Ryan" mean, anyway, though he figured it was best to talk about it later, after Barney left.

But now Lucille was wound up. "And you, Barney, don't call Reesh's beliefs 'Hindu shit.' You think you're the second coming of Socrates, but that comment was insensitive and racist. You're lucky Reesh didn't kick your ass."

"I'm just saying how it is," Barney protested. "And you can at least compare me to a real philosopher and not that pedophile."

Marty was tired of listening to Barney run off at the mouth. He also couldn't shake the image of Ryan Holt with his hand down Lucille's pants. "Hey," he said. "Back to the film, okay?" He started replaying the important scenes again, though it was clear that Barney and Lucille were losing interest.

He was just about to show them similar film clips from a ghost-hunting zine he subscribed to when Barney said, "No offense, dude, but I better track down Reesh. He's probably making a voodoo doll that looks like me."

Lucille looked about ready to explode again until Barney said, "Chill, Lucille. I'm just joking."

"I love you, Barney," she said. "But sometimes you can be a real asshole."

"I'll take that as a compliment," he said.

He was about to riff on some new topic when Marty pushed him toward the stairs, saying, "Go home and take a Xanax."

But Barney wasn't done yet. "Hey, weren't Robert and X-Ray supposed to be here?"

"Yeah," Marty said. "They showed up early, but X-Ray got freaked out by the film and said he had to go. You know how he gets. Robert left with him."

"X-Ray flipped out at the vigil, too," Barney said. "You ever think *he's* the ghost you're looking for? I mean, we hardly see the dude, and when we do, he goes catatonic and disappears faster than Justin Bieber at an AA meeting."

"X-Ray's okay," Marty said.

"I didn't say he wasn't. I mean, it can't be easy being black in this white bread town, unless your parents are Nigerian lawyers or Pakistani surgeons."

"Nothing like spouting a few racial stereotypes before you go," Lucille said.

"You saying I'm a racist when my best friend's from India?"

"I rest my case," Lucille said, laughing.

"Look, Barney," Marty said. "We know you're not a racist. You just talk too fucking much. Why don't you go home and chill out, and we'll meet up later?"

"Fuck you guys," Barney said, reluctantly climbing the stairs, then disappearing as Lucille yelled behind him, "We love you, Barney."

After his exit Marty debated whether to push the Ryan Holt thing with Lucille, eventually deciding against it. He wanted Lucille to go back to Alex's house with him, then maybe to a local cemetery—requests Barney had earlier refused—so he didn't want to get her mad.

Lucille started to look at the tape again while Marty rifled through some of his articles on ghost hunting and sorted lenses. He could feel Lucille shifting her focus from the TV to him. Finally she asked, "What are you going to do, Marty?"

"Well, here's the thing," he said.

"Oh, no." Lucille sighed. "Whenever you start a sentence that way, you end up doing something stupid."

"No, Lucille, whenever I start a sentence that way, I end up doing something interesting. Would you rather me spend my life taking pictures of fruit for Shaw's grocery flyers?"

"You'd probably make a better living than trying to film ghosts."

"So you're moving toward the dark side, too?"

Lucille waved him off. "Don't give me that dark side crap. It's so dramatic. You know I think you're a genius."

Marty stopped shuffling through articles. "Really? You've never said that before."

Lucille put down the remote. "What time are your parents coming home?"

"In about an hour."

She grabbed his hand and led him to the couch. "Will you cuddle with me for a while?"

"Just cuddle?"

"We'll see, but right now that's all I need."

Thinking about Ryan Holt, Marty wanted to do more than cuddle. "Sure," he said.

"Don't talk, though. I'm tired of all the talking you guys do."

"Okay," he said, stretching out next to her. She had a thin, hard body and small breasts. He wanted to make out with her but settled for breathing in her perfume. To Marty, she was flat-out beautiful. He never understood what she saw in him, but he was glad she had decided to stick around.

* * *

Marty knew that Lucille had a ten o'clock curfew on weekdays, so he met her at 9 p.m. on a beach a few hundred yards from Alex Youngblood's house. The bay was so flat and quiet that they could hear voices and the clash of dinner plates from a nearby house. They walked down the beach and veered off toward the fringe of a wooded area, where they set up Marty's camera on a tripod.

Lucille looked nervously around. "We're not on their property, are we?" she asked. "That would be really insensitive, Marty."

"We're okay here," Marty said.

"Is that camera new?" she asked, bending over and inspecting it.

"Yeah, it's a Sony camcorder with infrared capability."

"How much was that?"

"Dunno. It was a birthday present from my dad."

Lucille couldn't suppress a laugh.

"What's so funny?" Marty said.

"It's just that you and Barney always put down the 'rich kids' in town."

"So ..."

"So do you think there's some poor inner-city kid from South Providence who got a 'Sony camcorder with infrared capability' for his

50

birthday?"

"Not unless he stole one."

Lucille's head jerked back as if someone had shoved her. "Wow, Marty, I can't believe you said that."

"Yeah, that was pretty shitty, but can we just drop it and get these contraptions set up?" Marty burrowed through his backpack and pulled out a black box that looked like a computer modem.

"Another new toy?"

"Yeah," Marty said, proudly displaying it. "It's an electromagnetic field detector that picks up energy sources, so if nothing visible manifests itself, we can still tell if there are any paranormal phenomena around."

"I'd like to sue the people who made *The Conjuring*."

"I'm not done," he said, and he reached into his bag and extracted a dark red circular gadget. "This is a digital voice recorder so we don't have to write stuff down anymore. Later on, I can fiddle with it and see if it picked up any weird sounds. What's cool is that all this stuff's battery operated."

"Someone's been a busy boy," Lucille said, helping to set up his equipment.

When they were finished, Marty said, "Okay, let's start."

"Can't we skip this part?" Lucille said.

"Something strange happened at Alex's vigil, Lucille. Maybe he's trying to get in touch with us, but who knows if some evil spirits are getting in his way." Not giving her a chance to respond, he clasped his hands in prayer, looked up into the heavens, and said, "Dear Lord, what we are about to do, we do in the interest of science. We ask for your blessing and protection if our presence brings forth any minions of evil."

Lucille groaned.

Much to Marty's disappointment, for the next hour and a half nothing happened. But then, just as he was about to pack up, the EMF detector lit up.

"Some energy source must be close by," he said, eyeing the rim of the woods where puffs of smoke floated near some tall bushes.

"What's that, Marty?" Lucille said, sidestepping closer to him.

51

"Maybe paranormal smoke. That's when a spirit doesn't have enough energy to appear yet." Marty checked the camera, making sure everything was working properly, and when he looked up again, a black shadow passed near the edge of the woods, then moved toward them. There was a brief flicker of lights followed by a boom and a bright flash. After Marty's eyes readjusted to the night, the shadow came rushing at him and knocked him over. He tried to break free of the creature, surprised it could feel so human.

"Begone, spirit, begone," he yelled, punching the ghost in the gut.

"Jesus, Marty," a voice said. "You're hurting me."

Marty stopped fighting and struggled to his feet. Below him, dressed all in black, was a kid wearing a black ski mask, which he quickly tore off.

It was Barney.

"What an asshole," Lucille said, whacking Barney in the arm.

A big grin flashed across Barney's face. "But you have to admit, the cherry bomb was a nice touch."

Marty was trying to decide whether to break his EMF detector over Barney's head, but then the lights in Alex's house came on.

"Great," Marty said. "Let's get outta here."

All three of them packed up Marty's equipment, then trotted along a path near the woods until they came out onto the main road, pretty much winded. They stood under a lone streetlight as a Land Rover rushed by, almost grazing them.

"Fuckhead," Marty yelled.

"Asshole," Barney added, and then said, "What was that cool shit we just packed up?"

"That's all you have to say?" Lucille said. "Not even 'I'm sorry'?"

"It was a joke, Lucille."

"How about this for a joke, Barney. Some night when you're dead asleep I'm going to sneak into your house and stand over your bed with a butcher knife, and when you wake up to pee, I'm gonna scream and bury the knife about two inches from your face."

Marty started to laugh, which got Lucille laughing too. "Shh," he said, glancing around, not wanting to wake up the neighborhood.

Lucille looked at her watch. "I really have to get home, Marty."

"Me, too," Barney said.

Marty had other ideas, but this time he wasn't going to share them. "If I were you," he said to Barney, "I'd take the bike path. If any cops see you in that black ninja costume, they'll lock you up."

"Oh yeah," Barney said, "because, like, the bike path is safe. Just ask Alex Youngblood." Then he jogged away, whistling the opening theme from *The X-Files*.

Left alone, Marty decided to go for it. "You know, Lucille, I was thinking, since we're already out and the cemetery's only a few blocks away ..."

"No way, Marty. My dad will kill me if I don't get home. I'm already late."

"No, your dad's cool about anything that's interesting."

"So you know my dad better than me?"

Lucille's father taught journalism at Brown. He'd once told Marty that the only thing that could bring down the world was boredom.

"I'll settle it with your pops," he said. "You know he likes me."

Lucille hesitated, then grabbed her phone from the rear pocket of her jeans and handed it to him. "Let's test your theory about my dad."

As it turned out, Marty was right, so five minutes later they were on the bike path, heading toward a small cemetery dating back to the early eighteenth century. Marty chose it because it was old, rarely visited, and close by.

"Thanks," he said as they continued down the path.

"For what?"

"For being Lucille."

Lucille smiled. "You're not going soft on me, are you?"

"Never."

At that moment everything seemed perfect to Marty, yet he couldn't shake the image of Lucille and Ryan Holt holding hands and strolling down this same path. "Can I ask one more question about that Ryan guy?" he said.

"You can ask anything you want, Marty."

She walked a few paces ahead of him, and Marty hurried to catch up. "But you aren't going to answer me, are you?"

Lucille turned and smiled. "No, Marty, I'm not."

And that was that.

They continued toward the cemetery. Marty's backpack weighed heavily on his shoulders, but he didn't mind. Granted, the night, so far, had been another ghost-hunting bust, but no one would ever convince him that ghosts weren't real—maybe even watching over him, trying to decide if he was worthy of an appearance. Or perhaps they wanted to hurt him for intruding upon their afterlives.

Although the latter possibility spooked him, for some reason it also made him laugh—a laugh that reverberated through the night, reminding him of how Echo Pond had gotten its name.

X-RAY

I was night-fishing and pretty stoned when I heard the shot.

Next, I saw a yellow flash surprise the night—like a squadron of fireflies simultaneously igniting—but I didn't want to call the cops. I didn't want to draw attention to myself, considering what had happened to me and a guy named Ray last Christmas, not to mention that it was probably just some punks setting off an M-80 a few weeks before the Fourth of July. I was under this enormous tree limb that a kid named Shane had hanged himself from about four years ago, a kid everyone called an Outlier, though he always treated me decently, probably because I was an Outlier, too. Sometimes I feel invisible, like Captain Kirk in that old *Star Trek* episode where he comes back through the transporter as two Captain Kirks, one who's all evil and another who's all good. Like there's a wrestling match going on inside my head, and I don't have a clue who's going to win—a creepy feeling that fades only when I'm with Ray, who gave me a job during the summer and at Christmas breaks and promised to hire me after graduation, which made me feel older, almost normal, the opposite of how I am with kids at school, even nice ones like my friend Robert Hammersmith, because how can I explain to them all the terrible things I see every time I close my eyes? Images even my Xanax can't scare off, just like it couldn't stop that shot from rattling around in my head, so that last December with Ray could be happening now, or yesterday, because that's how it usually goes with me, the natural divisions of time, the past and the present, as indistinguishable as the sky right before daybreak, so that the story

I'm about to tell could be the reason for the shot I heard at the pond, or vice versa....

* * *

I'm waiting for Ray's call, halving my pills with a Swiss Army knife. I put one in my shirt pocket, another in the watch pocket of my jeans in case the old dread arrives, whereupon I'll swallow it and forget for a while, sometimes even becoming Ray, who right now is on the phone saying Linda told him to get another job or she'll dump him, and that she wants to get married and have a kid. Then I hear the phone go dead, then a honk outside, so I take another half and one more. I stumble downstairs, grabbing the railing, hugging the wall, my mom in her chair, asleep, the newspaper draped over her chest like a bib. Her mouth's half open as if practicing for death. Does she know what I'm capable of? That I stiffen when I think of these things, as if God Himself is reaching into my heart and saying, "X-Ray, that sleeping woman is trying to save you from yourself," because only He can see that black boat anchored in my head, its Captain, shotgun in hand, standing on its prow.

* * *

If my mom were to change into something, she'd be a large boulder, sanded smooth by years of wind and rain, and I'd draw a large heart on it with red paint.

* * *

We're in Linda's car, a brand-new red Ford Escort station wagon. The day she bought it Ray asks her, "You going upscale on me?" And Linda asks back, "What's upscale about an Escort?" Then Ray says, "Next, you'll be sleeping with a lawyer." Then Linda says, "Only if he gives back rubs like you, Ray." And that's how they get along, but not tonight, just Ray saying, "X-Ray, we're on our way." "To where?" I ask. "To some other planet," he says, giving that Ray laugh, full of confidence and trouble, mostly because of the Jack Daniel's wedged between his seat and emergency brake on this mid-January night, the roads as crystal clear as Ray's question: "You with me, X-Ray? You thought about it, man? Because this car has a mind of its own, and it's leading us to Louie's, where there will be princesses and trouble."

I'm hoping he's right. I'm hoping he's wrong.

* * *

If Linda were to change into something, she'd be a lilac bush, and I'd place her flowers in a jar next to my bed, and I'd never tell Ray.

* * *

Juney June is June and Alice is Christine, women we met at Louie's the night Ray named them, just like he named me—all of us actors in a movie written by yours truly, X-Ray.

Cast of Characters

RAY: About six feet tall. Handsome. Strong. Irish. Light brown hair tied back into a ponytail, green eyes, square jaw. Always wears blue jeans and untied work boots. Always wears flannel shirts. Often agitated.
ALICE, a.k.a. Christine: Almost as tall as Ray with short red hair, cut like Cleopatra's. Bright red lipstick, a red butterfly-shaped birthmark on her left cheek. Knee-high brown leather boots with zippers. Very often complains.
JUNE, a.k.a. Juney June, a.k.a. X-Ray's Juney June: Short and very thin. Purple hair spiked in sections. Tight blue T-shirt, tight black yoga pants, black high heels. Angelic.
X-RAY: Our hero. Usually nervous.

The Play

ALICE [sipping a White Russian]: I don't want to be called Alice.
JUNEY JUNE [sitting on a stool, hands between her legs]: I like Juney June—it sounds like a bird's song or a new kind of print dress.
RAY: We should go someplace. We should run off and get married.
ALICE: You really are nuts.

RAY [leaning over and blowing into her ear]: And you, Alice, really are sexy.

ALICE: You going to keep calling me Alice?

RAY: When I saw you drinking that White Russian, I was going to call you Maalox.

[Alice laughs.]

X-RAY [talking to himself]: Ray, if I could just be like you for a moment.

RAY: What was that, X-Ray?

X-RAY: Nothin', Ray.

JUNEY JUNE [to X-Ray]: Do you like Dwayne Johnson?

X-RAY: He's okay.

JUNEY JUNE: I've liked all his movies, but I never thought he looked like a rock. [Pause.] Whenever I say that, everyone laughs. Why didn't you laugh, X-Ray?

[X-Ray laughs, fingering a tiny white pill in his watch pocket.]

RAY: X-Ray, stop playing with yourself!

[X-Ray removes his hand from his pocket and waits for laughter to fade.]

ALICE: I want to know why you call him X-Ray.

RAY: I got drunk one night and decided we should give each other nicknames, and because he's like my alter ego, I named him X-Ray.

JUNEY JUNE: Like cutting your fingers and becoming blood brothers. That's cool.

RAY: Yeah, something like that. You know, you think like a poet, Juney June.

X-RAY [talking to himself]: You already have Alice, Ray, and Linda's at home. Let me have Juney June.

RAY: Stop mumbling, X-Ray. They're going to think you're weird.

JUNEY JUNE: I don't think he's weird.

ALICE [to Ray]: So what's your nickname, Big Shot?

RAY: We couldn't come up with one. I guess I'm too big of a personality.

ALICE: No doubt.

[Juney June and X-Ray go off to play a video game, which they never get to because Juney June keeps asking questions about Dwayne Johnson and movies with other black actors that X-Ray has never seen.]

JUNEY JUNE: You should go to college after high school, X-Ray. Anybody can go to a community college. I'm there now, taking this course called Genealogy, where you look up your family tree. I found out my family's from the same area as Tom Sawyer, so I'm thinking we might be related. Don't you ever want to look up your family tree?

X-RAY: No, not really, but I'm glad you like me instead of Ray.

JUNEY JUNE [laughing]: What an odd thing to say, X-Ray.

[X-Ray and Juney June go back to the bar, where Alice is showing Ray some postcards.]

JUNEY JUNE: I was just asking X-Ray if he ever wanted to look into his family tree.

RAY: If X-Ray has a family tree, it probably has a noose with his neck size hanging from one of its branches.

X-RAY [trying to change the subject]: Juney June says she thinks she's related to Tom Sawyer.

RAY: I thought he was a character in a book.

ALICE: A character in a book? You mean all this time you've been telling people you're related to someone in a book? That's as stupid as being related to a cartoon character.

[If Alice were to change into something, she'd be a weed or a plant with a big mouth, like a Venus flytrap.]

X-RAY [coming to the rescue]: A lot of characters in books are based on real people. I think that's what Juney June meant.

RAY: Yeah, that's right. I was probably wrong, anyway. I don't read books. [He grabs X-Ray by the arm and pulls him close.] Dig these postcards, X-Ray. Pictures of Niagara Falls in winter. Alice has this friend that moved there a month ago. Hardly anyone goes there in winter. Look what she writes on the back, "We want to see you, Alice, just show up." Just show up, X-Ray. What do you think about that?

X-RAY: I think you should bring Linda's car home.

ALICE: Who's Linda?

RAY: My sister.

ALICE: Won't she mind?

RAY: Not Linda, she's a good egg.

59

JUNEY JUNE: I certainly want to go. What do you think, Christine? I mean, Alice.

ALICE: I think it's a long way to go to get laid.

[X-Ray sighs, then feels in his jacket pocket for his bottle of pills.]

* * *

If Ray were to change into something, he'd be a big stray dog, like an Irish setter, and he'd love and protect you, and then one day he'd disappear like he never existed.

* * *

All four of us are crammed into a Ford Escort station wagon on the New York State Thruway for six hours in the middle of the night. Why didn't we count on the alcohol wearing off, or on Alice zipping her boots up and down, up and down, or on her saying, "I gotta pee again," or "Don't they have liquor stores on this road?" or "Why the hell did you have to finish the whole bottle of JD?" And finally, "If you call me Alice one more time, I'm gonna punch you." All this for six hours, her head one time vanishing into Ray's lap, but mostly just zipping and unzipping her leather boots, driving Ray a little bit crazy, until she says, "Did I tell you I slept with this old guy who slept with Elton John," which is when Ray veers into a rest stop outside of Syracuse.

"It's coffee time," he says.

The next time we see him he's on his cell phone outside the rest stop, and when he returns, Alice says, "Who the hell did you call?"

"Linda," Ray replies.

"You mean your sister?" Alice asks.

"No," Ray says, "I mean the woman I'm living with."

X-Ray duly notes the following:

1. Alice punches Ray in the arm and says, "You think you can treat us like fucking whores?"
2. Ray says, "What a mouth."
3. Alice says, "You weren't complaining about it an hour ago."
4. Ray says, "How do you plan on getting home from the Falls?"
5. Alice says, "The same way we got there, but with one less asshole

on board."

6. It begins to snow outside X-Ray's window, big wet flakes.
7. Juney June, who's fallen asleep on X-Ray's lap, awakens. X-Ray places his finger over her lips, saying, "Shh...."

Three hours of silence between Syracuse and Buffalo suggests that Ray and X-Ray will be alone in Niagara Falls.

* * *

Niagara Falls! My last image of Alice and Juney June—they're standing next to each other in front of a convenience store, Alice asking me to roll down my window, jamming her head into its opening. "You want a nickname, Big Shot?" she yells at Ray. "How about Jerk, Asshole, or Little Dick?" As she starts to walk away, I roll up the window, but she turns as if she's forgotten something. She wheels around and hikes up her skirt, then presses her ass against the glass. A big laugh, then she turns and faces me. "This has nothing to do with you, X-Ray. You're cool."

As Ray pulls away, I see Juney June for the last time. She's smiling, shrugging her small shoulders.

* * *

When Ray and I arrive at the American side of the Falls, the ground is snow-covered, the sky clear, the temperature feeling like zero. On the road to the tourist center something remarkable happens. Though we can't see the Falls, the mist is everywhere, and the trees seem made of glass, their branches and boughs encased in fine tubes of ice that shimmer beneath the sun.

"It's like we're in one of those glass paperweights," I say.

"I told you it'd be worth it," Ray says. "Totally exquisite, man. If only Linda were here."

When we reach the tourist center, we see one parked car but no people. The sidewalks haven't been sanded or salted, so we have to tiptoe to a rise overlooking the Falls. Ray goes first, grabbing my hand and pulling me with him. I feel myself go numb—not because of the rush of falling water, or the mist, or the noise, but the fear of tumbling

61

into the gorge, which seems as wide as one hundred football fields and as long as the finger of God. There are ice-covered stairs winding their way down to a scenic overlook, which is rimmed by a tubular metal fence, but we're blocked from the stairs by a chain and a sign that says this space is off-limits until spring.

Ray smacks the sign with the palm of his hand and says, "Fuck that," then drags me down the stairs, gripping the icy railing. When we reach the bottom, we're both too afraid to approach the fence. "This is crazy," Ray says, letting go of my hand and trying to crawl back up the stairs. I cling to the railing, not saying anything but knowing I can't let Ray get away, so I grab his legs and pull him down the first few steps. He probably thinks I'm scared, not knowing that it's come into my head to hurl us into the foamy, deafening noise below. He tries to calm me, then pushes me away, making us both slide toward the fence. When he realizes we're about to disappear under it and tumble into the gorge, he punches me in the face, then frees himself from my grip, slowly standing and trying to keep his footing as he drags me back to where we first started. "X-Ray," he yells, "what the fuck are you doing?"

* * *

What was it all about? you are probably asking. It was about a secret. Earlier that winter, in December, when I was close to eighteen, Ray and I killed a guy, though *killed* isn't the right word. We didn't beat up or shoot anyone, but the fact remains some guy is dead, and if it wasn't for us he'd be alive.

We knew there was going to be a snowstorm when we got to Louie's that night, but Ray drank hard anyway. As the snow fell, people began to leave early, but Ray had fought with Linda, so he wanted to keep drinking. I was worried because I had told my mother I was staying at Robert Hammersmith's house, and I was way underage, and I had a general gloomy feeling that something bad was going to happen. It was midnight by the time we left, and I asked Louie to call a cab, but Ray told us to go to hell. A few minutes later we were driving Linda's old 2010 Lincoln down the unplowed, deserted streets of Providence. In our defense, Ray wasn't driving fast, and he didn't fall asleep, and he was trying to be careful, and why would some guy be walking in the middle of the street at midnight during a snowstorm anyway, but he was, and before we could see him, we hit him from behind and watched as he flew into the air and tumbled over the back of the car.

Ray pulled over and said, "Jesus." Then he said, "Stay here," and he got out of the car. I could barely see him drag the body over to the curb, propping it up against a telephone pole. When he returned, I asked if the guy was alive, and he told me to shut up. As he started to pull away, I grabbed the wheel, and he said, "He's dead, man."

"How can you be sure?" I asked.

"You want to see for yourself?" And I shook my head, no.

We knew it was wrong, but we left anyway.

The next few days, the paper was full of the news. I learned that the guy had died of a broken neck. I learned all about him, how many kids he had, where he worked, where his wife worked, where he was going to be waked, and like Ray, I waited every day for a squad car to pull up and take me away. But it never happened, and Ray made sure the Lincoln was destroyed.

There's a guy I know who's into ghost hunting, his name's Marty, and he once told me that after people die they leave traces of themselves behind—like the energy that keeps memories from disappearing. If he's right, I often wonder if the guy we hit is still floating around, angry at me for participating in his death. Although that would make me sad, maybe even a little scared, I've also learned that, given enough time, a person can live with most anything.

*   *   *

The day after that flash at the pond, I found out that a kid named Alex Youngblood had been killed on the bike path near Echo Pond. He wasn't my friend, and had even bullied me a few times, yet I somehow ended up at a vigil outside his house with Robert Hammersmith and some other guys. Shortly after getting there, I started to feel anxious and ran off to a quiet spot in the woods where I could watch everything play out. I knew it was going to be a weird night from the moment they picked me up—Robert's face swollen from a fight he didn't want to talk about; kids acting like they were at a pep rally instead of a vigil; two guys I couldn't make out shoving each other over this girl named Patti, who I heard half the school had slept with. Eventually I found my way to a convenience store where I ran into my history teacher, who ended up buying me some Munchkins at a nearby Dunkin' Donuts. It wasn't until an hour or two later that I felt like myself, playing pool at a pizzeria with Robert, who couldn't stop talking about how he'd hung out with this rich girl named Missy Rogers after the vigil.

But I still felt anxious, like I was being stomped on by all the death and cruelty in the world. It was like I was waiting for … I'm not sure what, but I knew a question was being asked, knew there was an answer, though I couldn't quite glimpse it, even when I got back home, lighting a cigarette, contemplating the curved neck of that question, staring out the living room window as rain came down, the neighborhood asleep, my parents asleep, rain peppering the road, the front lawn spotted with puddles, telephone lines humped with beads of water. Then Silence, heavy with rain—inviting, bottomless Silence—came forth suddenly, and I embraced it, being in the question, surprisingly unafraid.

TAIL OF THE COMET

At 11 p.m. Lucille Gorski found herself standing in a faintly lit cemetery next to a monument proclaiming HEREIN LIES PHINEAS MCGEE, WHO LEFT WHEN HE HAD THE CHANCE.

"What do you think that means?" she asked her boyfriend, Marty, who was setting up his equipment.

"I guess the dude was glad to check out."

"Very funny, Marty, but don't push it. I've already done one ghost hunt tonight."

Lucille was referring to earlier when Marty had brought his ghost-hunting equipment to Alex Youngblood's house, a kid who'd recently been murdered on the bike path. Convinced he'd seen Alex's ghostly image wandering around at his vigil three nights before, Marty was hoping to catch Alex before he left for the Great Beyond.

In this sense, you could say Lucille's night actually began on the night of the shooting. She was about to plug into Cage the Elephant's first album when from her bedroom window she saw a flash spark in the distance, followed almost simultaneously by a loud bang. Once, about two years ago, she'd seen lightning, with its accompanying thunder, rend a tree. That's what she thought the flash was until she realized the night sky was quiet and star-filled. The next day when she heard that Alex had been shot, everything fell into place—the flash, the sound—because her house was no more than a quarter of a mile from where the murder occurred.

Murder. An unfamiliar word in Lucille's upscale community, though Marty seemed as excited about it as a coyote chancing upon roadkill. To Marty, a dead body meant a fresh ghost, and much to Lucille's unhappiness, Marty, her brilliant and—let's face it—cool-looking boyfriend, had decided to put all his energy into catching what he called Alex's "spirit force" before it broke its earthly coils.

"Are you going to help me, Lucille?" Marty asked, pointing to something he called an Electromagnetic Field Detector.

"I think you're way beyond help, Marty," she said.

He looked puzzled, as if trying to decide whether she was serious. Then his eyes left hers, traveling down and finally resting upon her Converse high-tops.

"You know, Lucille," he said matter-of-factly, "you really have great legs. I don't know why you always wear jeans."

It was not unlike Marty to unexpectedly shift gears between topics, so Lucille always had to be on guard. "You don't like the way I dress?" she said.

"What?"

"You were saying something about my legs."

"Yeah, I like them, but I'd like it better if we could get this stuff set up."

"Wouldn't you have a better chance of catching Alex's spirit if we went back to his house?"

"I'm not interested in just him anymore. I'm after the tail of the comet."

"I'm afraid to ask."

He assembled his tripod and placed his infrared camcorder on top of it. "It's like when a comet flames out and drags all this cool shit behind it. Well, when Alex passes through the Vortex, it follows that these dead people under all these tombstones might try to worm their way back into our lives. I guess I'm saying that because of the way Alex died, the natural order of things has been messed up. Don't tell me you can't feel it."

According to Marty, the Vortex, shaped like a funnel, was a gateway to the Other Side.

"Why would Phineas want to come back?" Lucille said. "He's been dead for three hundred years. Could you imagine him wandering into a Pilates class by mistake?"

"Very funny, Lucille. I find your irreverence for the dead sexy, though this probably isn't the best place to get them mad. They're not known for their sense of humor."

"Why's that?"

"Envy of the living, of course."

Lucille was about to challenge that answer but thought better of it. They'd already gotten her curfew extended, so she didn't want to prod Marty into one of his long paranormal lectures or they'd be there all night. Instead, she helped him set up his equipment, then awaited his usual invocation to the dead: "Dear Lord, what we are about to do, we do in the interest of science. We ask for your blessing or protection if our presence brings forth any minions of evil."

She sat down next to Phineas McGee's tombstone, and Marty turned some dials and then joined her. It was a beautiful night with low humidity—the full moon like the eye of God staring down at them.

"What are you expecting this time?" Lucille said, trying to seem interested, even though she knew nothing would happen for the next hour or so, and then they could go home.

"Something or nothing," Marty said, "but at least we're together, huh?"

"Yeah, Marty, you really know how to treat a girl."

"But you're not 'a girl.' You're Lucille. If you were 'a girl' you'd be afraid of cemeteries. You'd be home watching *Keeping Up with the Kardashians*. That's why I have trouble seeing you going out with that Ryan guy."

"Marty ..."

"I'm just saying."

"Well, don't."

Earlier that day Marty had discovered that she'd dated Ryan Holt, a kid Marty thought was a jerk, so since then he'd been harping on it, even though Ryan had been killed in a car accident last winter. Lucille knew what Marty wanted to know, and it bothered her that he thought, even for a moment, that she was his property.

"Okay," Marty said, "but you'll have to do penance for dating that guy, like telling me I have a large penis."

"Not going to work, Marty."

"What's not going to work?"

"If I tell you you have a large penis, you'll want to know what I'm comparing it with."

"You're a real piece of work, Lucille," Marty said, "and I mean that as a compliment."

Lucille grabbed his hand. He *really* was good-looking. He had deep-set blue eyes, a strong nose, and a slightly elongated chin, and when he smiled, a little dimple seemed to explode on his left cheek. He could get most anything with that smile, and she found herself jealous when he flashed it around other girls, especially ones like Dory Scheff.

Unlike Marty, Lucille was more than happy to battle almost anyone, as she did when she'd gotten into it with Dory at Alex's vigil. She didn't dislike Dory because she was rich or beautiful. She disliked her because Dory thought her beauty and money made her better than everyone else. Lucille knew that if she ever decided to wear her contacts and have her hair and nails done, she could be a real head-turner. That was made clear at the prom when Marty raved about her Japanese hairstyle with its long bangs that highlighted her eyes, and her tight red silk dress and red patent-leather shoes. Even Lucille noticed guys gawking at her, but what she loved about Marty was that after she went back to her black jeans, black Converse sneakers, and T-shirts, he was okay with it. They had made their statement to the cool kids without having to say a word.

"Shh," Marty said.

"Shh, what?"

"Look over by that stone wall."

Two eyes inflamed by moonlight appeared, and Lucille wondered if Phineas McGee had returned to drag them to wherever three-hundred-year-old dead guys live. But then the eyes moved slowly out of the woods, attached to the body of a gaunt coyote.

"Will it hurt us?"

"No," Marty said, "but at least I know my instruments are working." He pointed to the lights on the EMF detector, flashing on and off like bulbs on a miniature pinball machine.

The coyote sat down about thirty feet away, ignoring them. It glanced left, then right, as if it sensed a good meal scurrying through the wood's ground cover. Then it leapt over the stone wall and was gone.

Lucille locked her arm with Marty's.

"Don't worry. I think they're afraid of people," Marty said. "It's the guy wandering around who shot Alex that makes me nervous."

"Did you know Alex?" Lucille asked.

"A little. He was on my Pop Warner and Little League teams when we were kids."

"I didn't know you used to play sports."

Marty frowned. "They were fun back then. Now it's just the usual jerks trying to exclude people. My dad says the way to beat them is to outwork them, but why bother, especially when there are more interesting things to do. I didn't see myself getting eighteen guys together to play baseball after high school, anyway."

"That's how many guys are on the field?"

"You're kidding, right, Lucille?"

"No, I'm not."

"You mean your parents never made you play sports?"

"My mom wanted me to be a cheerleader."

Marty started to laugh.

"So you see the problem."

"Oh, yeah."

"You know, I don't mind talking about my mother," Lucille said.

"Well, that's a change."

"From what?"

Marty looked like he was trying not to smile.

"What's so funny?" Lucille said.

"Look, Lucille, every time we talk about your mom, you get severely pissed off." Lucille inched herself away from him. "I rest my case."

"You know what really stinks?" she said. "Sitting in a goddamn cemetery while you decide to give me a bad time about my mother."

"Actually, I didn't bring her up. What's going on, Lucille? Why don't you let it rip, so we can be quiet for a while. There aren't many rules to ghost hunting, but everyone agrees the dead won't appear if the living are making a racket."

Lucille felt herself smile. "You promise not to defend her?"

"I don't even know her."

"I love you, Marty, but you've got this thing about being nice to everyone. Some people are assholes, and you have to let them know it."

"That's your job, Lucille, and you're really good at it." He clasped his hands together as if in prayer, took a deep breath, and said, "So what's up with your mom?"

"My father says I need to spend more time with her."

"Might be a good idea."

"I can't stand her house or her new husband, and dig this, she's pregnant."

"Ah," Marty said. "It makes sense you're upset."

"Don't psychoanalyze me, Marty."

"I'm just saying."

Lucille felt herself about to cry and couldn't figure out why. "She's just so goddamn happy that it's not fair. My dad's a cool guy. I mean, he's a respected professor. Maybe he doesn't make a lot of money, but he's a great guy."

"It was probably more than money. People break up for a bunch of reasons."

"Not her. When they had fights, she'd say, 'Make more money.' One night she kept screaming it over and over again. My dad just sat in the kitchen with a glass of wine. I felt like punching her in the face. And so now she's got her rich guy—"

"And her new family," Marty interrupted.

"That's not the problem, Marty."

"Just putting it out there. Who knows, maybe a new kid will change things."

Lucille threw up her hands in frustration. "Obviously I can't talk to you about this, especially since your parents are so fucking happy."

Marty slid closer to her and placed his palm on her back, then gently scratched between her shoulder blades. "Well, I'll go with you if you want. Maybe I can beat up the guy."

They both laughed at that scenario, then sat quietly until they were surprised by an approaching bicyclist. The bike's lit headlamp came toward them, then stopped about fifty feet away. The rider got off and removed his helmet. Lucille couldn't distinguish his features, but he was tall and broad and appeared to be wearing a holster.

"He's got a gun," she whispered to Marty.

The man pointed a flashlight in their direction. "Just stay calm," he said.

Lucille tried to cooperate, but her heart felt a size too big for her chest.

"Is that you, Marty?" the man said, coming out of the shadows.

Marty stood. "Oh, hi, Mr. Watts."

Mr. Watts was a hunky ex-gym teacher who looked like Bradley Cooper. After two years of screaming at high school kids to do pushups, he had joined the local police force. He'd obviously been assigned to night patrol, most likely because of the shooting.

"Does your father know you're here, Marty?" Officer Watts said.

"No, but it wouldn't surprise him," Marty said. "Would you mind not shining that flashlight in my face, Mr. Watts?"

"Sure," Officer Watts said, turning off the light. He looked at the equipment, seeming to realize that they hadn't come to the cemetery to make out.

"I can explain," Marty said, and he calmly began a mini-lecture on ghost hunting.

Lucille expected Officer Watts to collapse into laughter, but he seemed interested, even asking Marty a few questions. When Marty finished, Officer Watts said, "You're a cool kid, Marty."

"Thanks."

"You always had interesting ideas in my health class, and you were polite. Some of those other guys could've used a kick in the ass."

"Thanks again, Mr. Watts."

"Having said that, I think you should pack up. I'll walk you kids home, or I can get a squad car if that's easier."

"Probably not a good idea to have a police car pull up to the town solicitor's house with his kid in it," Marty said.

71

Officer Watts nodded. "Yeah, you're probably right."

Lucille helped Marty to stuff the equipment into his backpack, and everyone was set to leave when Marty said, "I have to say something first. It'll probably sound strange."

This was the part of ghost hunting Lucille really hated. "You didn't say it at Alex's house," she reminded him.

"That wasn't a cemetery."

"Aw, come on, Marty," Lucille said.

Officer Watts seemed to be losing his patience.

"It's just a little prayer, Mr. Watts. Some ghost hunters believe that evil spirits sometimes follow people home from cemeteries, and not all of these ghosts are nice guys."

Lucille was waiting for Officer Watts to pull out his gun and put Marty out of his misery, but instead he looked uneasily around the graveyard. "Okay, so what's next?"

"We hold hands and I say a few words."

"Or we can just go home," Lucille said.

Lucille and Marty looked to Officer Watts for guidance. He probed the inside of his cheek with his tongue. "Okay, Marty, say your prayer, but this has to stay between us three."

Lucille and Marty agreed; then they all held hands, creating a small circle. After telling all evil spirits, in the name of God, to stay put, Marty lowered his head and said: "Saint Michael, the Archangel, defend us in battle. Be our protection against the wickedness and snares of the devil. By the power of God, cast into hell Satan and all other evil spirits, who prowl the world seeking the ruin of souls. Amen."

Lucille cringed as each word came out.

When Marty finished, they let go of each other's hands, and Officer Watts said, "You know, Marty, you should have your own TV show. You can really scare the hell out of people."

"Thanks, Mr. Watts," Marty said. He was beaming, and although Lucille felt like smacking him upside his head, more than anything she was glad someone was taking him seriously.

"Sure you don't want me to follow you?" Officer Watts said.

"We'll be okay," Marty said.

"Don't hang around, though."

"We won't," Marty said, and then he and Lucille grabbed his stuff and left the cemetery.

Later that night, a little after midnight, Marty called Lucille. She was sitting on her back porch, still hyped up from the visit to the cemetery. She was watching a *Stranger Things* episode on her tablet as mosquitoes unhappily vanished into a nearby bug zapper shaped like a lantern.

"Just wanted to thank you for tonight," Marty said.

"You don't have to do that."

"I know I'm a pain in the ass, but I really think I'm going to do something important someday."

"But not with ghosts, right?"

"I dunno. I just don't want you to think I'm an idiot." There was a long pause, and then he said, "I guess I'm trying to say I love you, Lucille."

"Even if I made out with Ryan Holt?"

"I'm serious, okay?"

"Sorry, Marty. I'm just not used to you talking like this."

"But I mean it. Right now, I'm kind of angry you can't be here and spend the night."

Lucille knew exactly how he felt. "I love you, too, Marty, but can we leave it at that? Sometimes talking about this stuff ruins things."

"You really are something, Lucille."

"Yeah, all I have to do is figure out what it is."

After the conversation Lucille sat for a while. A hurt that had morphed into a dull ache over the last few years was rising again deep inside her. Her mother's house was only a fifteen-minute walk away. She knew that what she was about to do would make her feel worse. But she was, after all, Lucille.

First she checked to see if her father was asleep. Then she threw on a black hoodie. She didn't want to take the sidewalks or side streets at midnight. That was a sure way to run into Officer Watts again, and she feared he wouldn't be so laid back this time. So she jogged onto a path that cut through the woods behind her house and ended a block from her mother's. From any place on the path, houses were no more than fifty yards away. Worst-case scenario, she could run to one of them. And from what? A coyote? A fisher cat? A stray dog she might spook?

The night had cooled off, so she pulled the hood up over her head, glancing periodically to the left or right. Dead leaves and twigs crunched under her sneakers. She heard a dog bark and the squawk of a window being lowered. The first part of her walk was straight and level, but then she reached a small incline and a bend that was dimly lit from the backyard floodlights of nearby houses. When she made the turn, she was surprised by a large kid with a shaved head who was sitting on the ground with his back against a tree, drinking from a six-pack of beer.

"Well, well, well," the kid said, standing up. It was Adam Igoe. He was a football player, a guy Lucille thought looked like one of those G.I. Joe action figures. He was wearing jeans and work boots and nothing but a plain white T-shirt on top. He raised the bottle of beer to his lips in such a way that his right bicep flexed. She almost laughed at his macho posturing, but even she was afraid of Adam. All he needed were a few tattoos of snakes on his head and he'd be ready for the World Wrestling Federation after graduation.

"Don't worry, I'm not going to hurt you," he said.

"I'm not worried," Lucille said.

"Gorski, right?"

"Yeah."

"You know what I remember about you?"

"Nope."

"Before you started going out with the film guy, we were both at this party when one of my friends grabbed your ass and you punched him in the face."

Lucille smiled, remembering the incident, but she wasn't sure where he was going with this.

"You want a beer?" he said, trying to be friendly.

"No, I'm in a hurry."

"Where're you goin'?"

Oh, what the hell. "To my mother's."

"Well, Gorski, let me finish this beer and I'll walk you outta these woods." He took a long suck on his bottle, then tossed it next to the unopened ones.

"You going to leave the rest here?" she said.

"No, I'll come back later."

"Aren't you afraid someone will steal them?"

"No, you and me are the only ones crazy enough to be here after midnight."

So there she was, Lucille Gorski, being escorted by a kid who was only a few genes from being a Neanderthal.

She and Adam never said a word until they reached her destination. She thanked him, and with everything else that had happened that night, she wouldn't have been surprised if he knelt down and kissed her hand.

"You're okay, Gorski," Adam said. "If anyone ever fucks with you, let me know."

Lucille said she would, then watched as he disappeared into the darkness to head back to his stash.

A minute later she found herself in her mother's backyard. All the lights were off, so she sat next to a shed that had a shovel leaning against it. She wrapped her arms around her knees and thought about the couple sleeping inside, imagining her unborn sibling coming to life inside her mother's womb.

She was angry and sad at the same time, wanting to leave but unable to move. She was surprised when a light came on in the living room, and then another, and another, until she could spot her mother pouring a glass of water from the kitchen faucet. She was wearing a thin white nightgown that broke above her knees. Lucille watched as her mother bent over, then rubbed her stomach with her free hand before walking toward the kitchen window and looking out into the backyard. She seemed to be staring right at Lucille, but darkness was Lucille's friend that night.

After finishing the glass of water, her mother sat at the kitchen table, and Lucille wished she could see her face better. Was she happy, sad, or just tired?

Having seen enough, Lucille stood to leave. Halfway up, she got momentarily dizzy and nearly fell to her knees, surprised by a grief she could no longer ignore. She felt like crying, but even more than that she wanted her mother to hug her and to never let go.

Oh, how she wanted that.

But she was Lucille Gorski, and Lucille Gorski would never give in.

FLAMENCO

Sometimes when my friend Adam and I get bored (which isn't hard in this stupid town), we meet at midnight behind the supermarket and drive old golf balls into its concrete wall, listening to them explode like firecrackers.

That's what the shot sounded like, though louder.

At first I thought it came from those hunters who'd been pissing off local yuppies by deer hunting a few hundred yards from their property. But who knows, maybe some poor bastard got sick of his manicured lawn and perfect family and put a bullet in his head. Whatever, it sure got my dad's attention, almost knocking him off his recliner, which is saying a lot.

`"What was that?"

"Probably the sound of one of Patti's boyfriends shooting up the neighborhood," I said, trying to get under his skin.

"You can't talk like that about your sister," he said.

"Just hard to believe we're sitting here when we know what she's up to for once. Seems like a good time to make a point."

"At least she's using her talent," he said.

"Unfortunately, that talent's going to get her pregnant."

"Remember, Frank, this is my house."

"And a man's home is his castle," I sang, almost adding that while the king was downing a few beers and wondering whether a fat slob of a first baseman was going to strike out or hit a home run, El Cobra, some thirty-something phony, was in the back room of a dumpy bar in

Warren having his way with Patti.

But I tried to be reasonable.

"If she could sing, this might make sense," I said, "but she shouldn't even be in that place. She's only seventeen."

"That never stopped *you*," he said, referring to the last time he threw out my fake ID. "Just give me a cigarette," he added, shaking his head.

I looked at him, seeing more of myself than I wanted to. People always said we looked alike; they couldn't even distinguish between our voices on the phone. I wanted to move out, but someone had to hold things together.

"I just want her to be happy," he said sadly.

"Well, we can always introduce her to guys. We already know her type: middle-aged wannabe rock stars, or rich kids looking for a good time. Maybe we can buy fedoras and drive around in a shiny pink Hummer."

"What?"

"Pimps, Dad."

He stood and threw the unlit cigarette onto the floor. "You talk like a pig about your sister. What's your problem?" He stuck a gnarled index finger into my chest, pushing me backwards. "You want me to beat up the guy?"

"His name's El Cobra. The Snake. You get the metaphor?"

He took a run at me, grabbing my shirt and shoving me against the wall. "Even though you're Patti's twin, you're nothing like her. You've always talked like we got the wrong kid at the hospital, like you're the kid of some junkie, because that's how you think—junk, crap, and more junk. You just make it sound better because you're in college now. Did you meet this El Cobra, you big jerk? He was polite. He was a gentleman." He loosened his grip and collapsed onto the recliner.

I adjusted my shirt. "Let me tell you something about El Cobra. I've been doing some checking. He's Italian but tells everyone he's Spanish and owns a villa in Europe. He's been divorced twice, has three kids from those marriages, and is currently shacked up with some poor girl who used to sing in his group. He knocked her up, Dad. The guy's thirty-six."

His eyes widened. "You sure about this?"

"You think I'd lie?"

"Jesus," he said. "We've got to get her out of there, Frank."

On the drive to Toucan's, the club where Patti was singing, he thanked me for being honest about El Cobra, and I felt a little guilty, though it wasn't as if I had totally lied. I was convinced that the truth about El Cobra was worse than anything I could make up. Granted, I hadn't met him and didn't know if he'd been married, but I knew my sister's type well enough to be pretty sure my guesswork was solid. The important point was that if I wanted to rescue Patti, I needed the old man with me.

When we got to Toucan's I was surprised that El Cobra's performance was sold out, so the bouncer wouldn't let me in without a ticket. I had a notion to return to the car and tell Dad, who had decided to wait outside, that at this very moment Patti was baring her breasts on stage to assorted drunks, which would've made him break down the door. But I didn't want to push my luck.

Still, I had to deal with the bouncer, who had the biceps of Batman and the face of an iguana. I was going to tell him he had a seventeen-year-old girl performing in the bar that night, but instead I calmly explained that I was the brother of one of the great flamenco singers of all time, who was currently performing with El Cobra and who had promised to leave me a ticket at the door. He looked at me as if I were a bug he was considering for dinner, then he eventually let me in, but not before saying, "If you screw up, Jack, you're out on your ass."

I showed him my new fake ID and said, "If a stocky old guy looking like the Avenging Angel of Death storms the front door, tell him I'll be standing by that big speaker on the left."

He looked suspiciously at me, trying to decide if I was ridiculing him, which I was. A muscle twitched in his left cheek; he opened his mouth, displaying a blackened set of teeth only a horse doctor could appreciate.

"I'm watching you," he said. "I'm watching you."

I smiled, thinking I could take him if push came to shove. For one thing, I'm big and strong. I'm sure I would have been some big, strong, dumb jerk laying bricks the rest of my life if I hadn't scored off the charts on standardized exams, which got me an early-admission ticket to college. But I'm also invincible when I'm righteous, and I was feeling very righteous that night. I didn't want to save Patti from herself, which was impossible, but I was going to make it clear to El Cobra and to any other fast dick in town that to screw with my sister was to screw with me. If I could make that point with my wits, all the better. If not, I was more than willing to fight someone.

Once inside Toucan's, I headed to the bar and bought a Rolling Rock, then walked over to a large speaker, looking for a table. Unfortunately, the ones in front were reserved for flamenco aficionados, phonies who had decided to be someone else for a night. I was surprised to see Campbell McVeigh, a kid from my old high school, slamming down a beer with a few of his rich friends, which meant someone was making a fortune selling fake IDs. Last year I'd gotten stoned with him a few times, but I didn't like him, and he had a fascination for guns that was beyond creepy. He was the kind of jerk Patti attracted, one of those rich jocks who think they can treat people like shit. He waved to me and I nodded, watching as he momentarily disappeared into the swirling smoke. In the four corners of the room, the management had set up miniature searchlights that slowly swept across the audience, occasionally crisscrossing one another, cutting swaths of light through the smoke.

The rumble of small talk quieted down, and to my right I saw El Cobra's entourage hugging a cheap wood-paneled wall as they struggled through the crowd onto the stage. They were led by El Cobra himself, waving his guitar over his head, acknowledging the applause. Some patrons yelled out Spanish phrases they stole from old Zorro movies, and I joined in with a few yips and yaps of my own.

Patti was wearing a thin white cotton dress, so whenever the searchlights discovered her, you could see the outlines of her bra and panties. Her long blond hair bounced on her shoulders as she pranced around on the stage. I knew she'd attract attention from the male clientele. I knew that when these phony Chiquita bananas spotted her, they'd let out a collective sigh that only her beauty could elicit.

She was going to perform with two dark-skinned women, and I had to admire El Cobra's taste. At their feet were instruments—pieces of metal and wood—that I had never seen before, and when the Snake Man started to play, the two women shook and banged them, yelping like a bunch of wounded coyotes. El Cobra himself stood at the microphone fingering and smacking his guitar. He was shorter than I'd expected, his hair the color and texture of Patti's.

After a few songs El Cobra asked Patti to join him, introducing her as a new member of the group, kissing her paternally on the cheek. That's when Campbell appeared again, waving a Rolling Rock over his head, then bowing at the waist, as if in solemn respect. El Cobra smiled, but I wasn't fooled by these pleasantries.

He continued to speak about his home in Spain, explaining how the next song, which he'd written for Patti, was inspired by the "untamed" women of his region. When Patti approached the microphone, he began to pick feverishly at his guitar, while she howled and gyrated before him until it seemed like the whole room was about to erupt into fornication. I was trying to decide how to handle the situation when I was saved by Campbell, who was clapping and jumping up and down as if his feet were on fire.

How could I not laugh at this spectacle?

At first Patti and El Cobra attempted to continue, but then, as if suddenly hearing the familiar sound of my laughter, Patti stopped yelping, while El Cobra joined her at the microphone, holding his guitar at his side like a staff. As they squinted into the house lights, I could feel the growing silence in the audience, but as long as Campbell was in sight, I couldn't stop laughing.

Visibly pissed off, El Cobra asked the stage manager to shine a light on the blasphemer of flamenco (me), and I was temporarily blinded, he and my sister becoming distant silhouettes. That's when I heard El Cobra—not El Cobra the famous flamenco guitarist, not El Cobra the Latin lover, but El Cobra the dago from North Providence—yell, "What's the matter with you, buddy?"

"Snake Man," I yelled back, "can you repeat that in the native Spanish of your homeland?"

I was caught off guard by what happened next. El Cobra, this pygmy-sized gaucho, dropped his guitar and charged me from the stage, with Patti close behind. The stage manager, noticing the action, shifted a different set of lights onto the streaking guitarist and his enraged lead singer. When El Cobra got a few feet from me, I reacted instinctively and punched him in the face. He went down hard and lay motionless on the floor. Instead of coming to his aid, Patti barrelled into me, wrapping her arms around my waist and trying to push me backward. I raised my half-finished bottle of beer over my head and tried to hold her tightly to my chest with my other arm, but she fought herself free, swiping an empty bottle off a nearby table, and hitting me in the face with it. I felt a warm scar of blood snake its way down my cheek, but instead of getting mad, I smiled. She probably would've stabbed me with the jagged edge of the bottle if the bouncer hadn't intervened, who passed her to another bouncer before rushing me himself. He'd obviously been looking forward to this confrontation, but much to his disgust, I went limp. I wasn't afraid of him, but I had accomplished my mission and didn't see any reason to fight.

A few minutes later, I was on my ass on the sidewalk outside Toucan's, my beer still in hand, blood trickling down my cheek, old Iguana Face smiling down at me as if he'd just finished his third Big Mac. "You're an asshole, Jack," he said, acting very much the victor, which he would've been if not for the crazed King of Dudek's Bowling Lanes, alias Dad, who at that moment was charging him like a psychotic elephant.

It was no contest.

Dad and the bouncer went hurtling into the smoke-filled twilight of the bar. I saw the event from Dad's point of view: he's stewing in the car for over a half an hour when he looks up and sees his son dragged out with a head wound.

Knowing that Dad could take care of himself, I walked back to the car and leaned against the hood. Sure enough, about five minutes later, he stumbled out of Toucan's, dragging Patti behind him, followed by Campbell McVeigh and his crew, who were still holding their beer bottles and laughing their asses off. I was about to go after Campbell when my father pushed Patti into the back seat and told me to get into the front. On the drive back, Patti told him what had happened, and as she spoke I sensed my father looking sideways at me. Later, at home, he sat with her, half chastising her, half comforting her. I went into the bathroom and closed the door behind me, working on my face with a washcloth and some peroxide. I was almost done when the door opened and Patti appeared. She grabbed the washcloth and rubbed it deeply into my open cut. Although it stung mightily, I never blinked, never took my eyes off her until I sensed my father standing in the doorway.

"You're a bastard," he said.

I felt sorry for him, but I knew that he'd eventually understand the soundness of the rescue, that someone had to defend what little dignity our family had left.

For the next couple of days we didn't see much of Patti, which was good because we were afraid of what she might do next, especially since she'd heard that one of Campbell's friends, Alex Youngblood, another rich kid she'd briefly hung out with, had gotten killed on the bike path the night of the Toucan fiasco.

That explained the shot my dad and I had heard. Still, I tried to keep a close eye on her, even following her to a vigil for the kid, where I got into a shoving match with my old history teacher, who I'd recently discovered had been calling her at home. Jesus! After that, I stopped at Subway and ate a steak sandwich before heading off to a tiny beach area at Colt State Park, where I climbed to the top of a high slide overlooking Narragansett Bay. To my right, I could see lights from the mansions that rimmed the coastline, and I tried to think back to happier times, knowing there were no happier times.

Ten years ago, one damp April morning, the cops discovered a middle-aged woman face down in Echo Pond. As she floated close to shore, a tree branch had reached out and hooked her by the rosary she wore around her neck. The woman was my mother; the rosary was from some shrine in Yugoslavia. The last person to see her, a clerk at Rite Aid, said she had stumbled in drunk from the pouring rain and had given him a holy card of Saint Theresa. "Praise be to Jesus," she had said on her way out.

The police found no evidence of foul play. To them she was just another drunk, another nutcase. When my father went to identify her, in one of the stupidest moves of the century, he brought Patti with him. She was only seven at the time, yet no one stopped her from following him into the room.

Unbelievable! I say. Fucking unbelievable!

GHOSTS

To Jamie the shot that disrupted her normally peaceful neighborhood was just another muffled gasp from the stupefied world she currently inhabited, something to be endured until nightfall when Ryan came to her, sometimes appearing unexpectedly at the foot of her bed, other times drifting through an open window shrouded in a silky pale mist. He was always shirtless, wearing nothing but tight-fitting blue jeans, his chest glowing like that of a Christ figure she'd seen on the cross while traveling with her parents in Venice.

He would stand silently until she approached, then remove her nightgown and kiss her softly on the lips. His lips were hot, and when he held the kiss too long she thought she might burst into flames. After the kiss he'd sit on her bed and draw her to him, touching her breasts, then slowly making love to her. He never blinked, the irises of his eyes a bright dandelion yellow.

The truth was, he was a more thoughtful lover dead than alive. While alive, he could be rough with her, and he'd get angry when she refused to say things she felt were embarrassing. But now he was gentle and attentive. One night she asked what had made him change, but during those early visits he never spoke, as if death allowed him only certain privileges. So she contented herself with his silent lovemaking, after which he'd stroke her hair, then gently massage the six-inch scar disfiguring the hollow of her lower back.

Ryan had been dead for three months. It happened at the end of February when they'd gone to a party. He had his night license and his father's car, and everything was fine until one of the jocks got drunk and tried to hit on her. Ryan thought Jamie had been flirting with the guy, which wasn't true, but then Ryan had always been jealous. It was a trait her parents had hated; her mother, a psychologist, had called it "controlling."

Although her parents were supportive after the accident, they were, Jamie knew, secretly glad Ryan was gone. Now she no longer cried on the phone at odd hours of the night or avoided her friends. But what they didn't know was that since Ryan had returned, Jamie had no interest in those friends—or anything else, for that matter. All she thought about was being held and loved, knowing she was close to all things heavenly, for certainly that was where Ryan had come from.

Or so it seemed, because as the months wore on, she noticed changes in him. The glow that originally cloaked him faded into a grayish mist, and his skin, at first an alabaster sheen, took on an almost sickly shade of beige. That's when she feared she was losing him.

She didn't ask herself how much time he had left. She didn't ask if continuing to make love to a ghost was unnatural. She feared that even raising that question might cause Ryan to be dead for good, and that was unthinkable. It would have helped to confide in someone about his visits, but who would've believed her?

Still, one night, she almost took that chance.

Her friend Dory Scheff decided to have a slumber party for her eighteenth birthday, and Jamie couldn't beg off going. In a way she wanted to see her friends again, but what would Ryan do when he discovered she wasn't home? All night, through pizza and ice cream and cake, through small talk and Megan Flaherty, another one of Dory's friends, constantly calling Dory a slut for wanting to date a boy named Alex Youngblood, Jamie wondered if Ryan had arrived.

"Dory and The Gunslinger," Megan kept saying, using the nickname Alex's friends had given him. "Dory and The Gunslinger. What a slut!"

"He's not so bad," Dory said.

Megan kept shaking her head. "But what a stupid nickname. Like he'd even know what to do with his thing. Gasp!"

They all laughed, though Jamie couldn't help but be distracted, because Alex was the jock who had made Ryan so jealous that after the party he ran a stop sign at the corner of Wellington and Country Road at exactly the same time a pickup truck equipped with a snowplow passed by. Ryan was killed instantly, Jamie miraculously ending up with only a deep gash in her back and on-and-off headaches that still persisted. In the beginning, she wondered if Ryan's visits might be hallucinations, if nerves had been severed or brain tissue destroyed in the accident, so that Ryan was no more than a clump of damaged neurons misfiring.

But could hallucinations touch and feel and speak? Could they make love?

Looking at and listening to her friends, she felt older and wiser than them and couldn't wait for the night to end. Perhaps she could sneak out for a few hours, she thought. But she'd forgotten that girls stay up late at slumber parties. She'd forgotten how much gossip could be shared, how many stories told that never happened. She should have left Ryan a note. What would he think? So she tried to act interested, half listening until, like everyone else, she fell asleep.

The next night she lay in her own bed, watching the hours pass as ice melted in a cup of water next to her bed. At 2 a.m. she went to her window and remained there for more than an hour. She gazed at the moon moving slowly across the horizon as if pulled by a string.

Because Ryan appeared at many different hours, there was still hope. But were there rules in the afterlife she was unaware of? Perhaps Ryan's travels depended on Jamie making love to him every night. Perhaps her absence alerted a higher authority that Ryan's time with a living, breathing girl was over.

Finally she crawled into bed and fell asleep, only to awaken with Ryan looming over her.

He was not happy.

"Where were you last night?" he asked, and Jamie told him about the slumber party.

He looked disgusted. "Yesterday could've been our final night," he said, "and you decided to hang out with Dory. Were there any guys there?"

"No."

"You sure? I can leave for good, if that's what you want."

She felt lightheaded and afraid. "You know I couldn't bear that."

"I'm not so sure."

She drew her knees to her chest and began to cry, but Ryan wouldn't stop.

"So what should I do?" he said.

She reached out to him. "Just come to bed."

And he did.

Later, after they had made love, she promised never to be away again, though, secretly, she found herself imagining ways she might end his visits. Unlike in the beginning, he seemed anxious now and more preoccupied with the real world, always demanding to know what had happened in school and whom she'd spoken with. He was particularly interested when he learned that Alex Youngblood had been murdered on the bike path, which accounted for the muffled shot she had heard that night, though what he really wanted to know was if Alex's death made her sad.

"Of course I'm sad," she said, "but I hardly knew him."

"No one would've thought that at the party."

She didn't answer for fear of making him angry again. And when she told him there was going to be a vigil outside Alex's house, he thought they should go.

"You can do that?"

"Only if you want me to."

"But like I told you, I hardly knew Alex."

"We'll see if that's true when we're there."

"You mean Alex isn't dead?"

"No, he's dead, but that doesn't mean he's gone or that he won't be interested in you."

"Will I be able to see him?" Jamie asked. "Will others be able to see you?"

"I'm pretty sure just you. It has something to do with the accident, with something that happened to you."

"I'm not dead, am I," she asked, her voice cracking, "and all of this is just a dead girl's dream?"

He laughed. "No, you're not dead, though sometimes I wish you were."

She didn't know if he wished that out of love or if he had a darker motive. But two nights after she heard the shot, she found herself with other kids on the front lawn of Alex's house holding an unlit vigil candle given to her by Missy Rogers, the girl who had organized the event. Jamie tried to stand apart from everyone, wondering when Ryan would come.

The group was small, maybe thirty kids, and she was surprised to see Megan and Dory there. Only four or five of Alex's jock friends came, and the rest were mostly girls, except for three geeky boys who kids called The Three Stooges. They were about ten feet from her, so she could hear their conversation. Strangely, they were arguing about reincarnation. One of them, a boy named Barney, joked that Alex would probably come back as a football, and a short boy with a large bruise on his face, whose name she thought was Robert, said he didn't think that was very funny.

That's when Ryan emerged from the woods that bordered Alex's house.

He was not alone.

Behind him were three boys, shirtless and pale, along with some girls in sheer white cotton dresses with plunging necklines. Barefoot, the girls seemed to glide above the dew-covered grass, their hair flowing behind them as if caught by a light breeze. One particular girl stood out among the others. Her skin was the color of moonlight, her hair raven black. Some of them appeared sad, others startled to find themselves there, but the beautiful girl seemed in complete control, as if used to such vigils. Instead of forming a group by themselves, the dead dispersed among the living, examining them with a mixture of curiosity and envy. Jamie looked to see if anyone else had witnessed their arrival, but it was clear no one had.

Ryan watched them, then moved toward Jamie, eventually standing next to her.

"I didn't think you were coming," Jamie said. "Who are those other kids?"

"The recently dead," Ryan said. "They've come to take Alex and some of us whose time is up. Only *she* knows for sure," he added, pointing to the beautiful girl.

"But *you're* not leaving, are you?"

"I don't know," Ryan said. "I knew I had to be here, just like I knew I had to see you again."

He looked scared, and Jamie was about to console him when she sensed another presence behind her. It was Missy Rogers.

"Thanks for coming," Missy said. "It's so sad."

"Yes, it is," Jamie agreed.

"Here," Missy said, lighting Jamie's candle and then the candles of the other kids grouped around her. Soon the night's darkness glowed with fingernails of light, which seemed to give form and substance to the dead.

A few seconds later Alex appeared on his porch. His presence made Ryan laugh. It was a sinister laugh Jamie had never liked. Alex sat and rested his elbows on his knees, his palms cradling his chin. He was examining the crowd, but who could guess what he thought of this gathering? Everyone stood quietly for a moment, and then a few jocks started laughing and chasing each other around with their candles until Missy Rogers asked them to be quiet.

That's when two of the dead girls approached Alex. Blond, beautiful, and angelic, they were floating a few inches above the ground, reaching out to him. He looked sad, sadder than Jamie could imagine any living or dead person ever being. At first he refused their help, but then he gave in, momentarily hovering between the two girls as if realizing there might be some benefits to being dead.

Jamie turned back toward Ryan, but he was gone. Eventually she saw him under a streetlight, talking to the beautiful dead girl. The girl smiled at Jamie, then grasped Ryan's hand, and Jamie knew what that meant. She ran toward them, her candle extinguishing itself on the way. By the time she reached the streetlight, both the girl and Ryan were gone. She frantically searched Alex's backyard, finally spotting them right before they entered the woods. Ryan was still holding the girl's hand, trailing her like a little boy. He waved at Jamie, appearing more confused than afraid. And then, in what seemed like seconds, all the dead, including Ryan, faded into the night, and Jamie began her long walk home.

She refused to fall asleep that night, never taking her eyes off the bedroom window. But Ryan never appeared. She waited for the old anguish to set in, what her favorite poet, Emily Dickinson, had called the Hour of Lead. But that stupor never arrived. She would miss Ryan's visits and the softness of his skin, but she had become fearful again, too, and she wouldn't miss that. Remembering how the raven-haired dead girl had smiled at her, she wondered if, in a way, the girl had been sent from the grave to save her.

The next morning at the breakfast table her mother touched her wrist and said, "Are you okay, sweetie? We heard you crying a few nights ago but felt you wanted to be alone."

Jamie looked around the kitchen—at a vase of roses and a pitcher of milk resting harmlessly on the counter, at a reproduction of Degas's dancers hanging on the wall. Everything suddenly seemed so real. She was even looking forward to going to school. She wanted to tell Dory not to be surprised if Alex came back, and if he did, not to make love to him or to think for a second that death might make him a better person.

She smiled at her mother. "It was just a night terror," she said.

"Wow, you haven't had those since you were a little girl."

"Yeah," Jamie said, "but don't worry. I'm going to make sure it never happens again."

LA CUCARACHA HUMANA

Barney Roth was so lost in photographs of cockroaches that he barely heard the shot that woke up half his neighborhood—a sound that wouldn't break through his cockroach thoughts until ten minutes later, when he'd say to himself, "What the fuck was that?"

That's what it was like to be inside Barney Roth's head.

There was something wrong with his La Cucaracha. He had wanted to create a symbol to tick off the fashionably contented, mindless occupants of his town. The Pilates moms pecking one another on the cheek while sipping Very Berry Hibiscus Refreshers at Starbucks. The Episcopalian do-gooders distributing hand-me-down Brooks Brothers polos to homeless families that their banker husbands had put out onto the streets. And especially his nitwit classmates, both rich and poor, who, like lobotomized zombies, embraced their antiseptic, safe lives.

Yeah, Barney was feeling particularly alienated lately, so what better symbol to choose than La Cucaracha, The Cockroach—to most decent people, a dirty scavenger, a night stalker who could frustrate even the most determined exterminator. Just the thought of a cockroach could make girls squeal and grown men run for brooms. But that wasn't the only reason Barney chose it for his alter ego. The cockroach was also persistent. It could adapt and thus survive, and Barney prided himself on those traits.

So what started as a joke became a passion, and he spent many nights envisaging the creature he would eventually draw or paint all over town. At first, his canvases were the walls of structures no one cared about, like the abandoned brick building at the cove where kids went to drink and make out. But then he moved on to bridges and supermarkets and convenience stores before finally getting the nerve to paint La Cucaracha on the high tan wooden fences of the rich while they escaped to their weekend beachfront houses.

That's when he graduated from being an oddity to a public nuisance, though no one, not even his friends, knew that he was the artist behind La Cucaracha. In fact, only a few art teachers from middle school were aware of Barney's talent. Although he had a lot of ideas he'd spout to anyone who'd listen—ideas on politics, history, rap music, even on the existence of God—he was pretty insecure about his artistic abilities.

His early graffiti was realistic, just a giant bug about a foot long and a foot wide with LA CUCARACHA scrawled below it in a simple, basic font. Nothing flashy, but still pretty offensive, because he'd added some serious puke-green tints to La Cucaracha's thorax, then painted a poisonous yellow line down its back. Purists, kids who knew Spanish, suggested the unknown insect artist didn't know what a cockroach looked like. Others, who had no idea what *cucaracha* meant, thought the creature was a beetle. Still, everyone, including the cops, wasn't very happy about its presence, and that was, after all, what Barney had wanted.

At least for a while.

But it didn't take long until everyone got used to La Cucaracha, proving Barney's theory that in our "current stupefied me-obsessed culture" (his words), people were by nature ADHD and constantly needed something new. And that's when—and this was a real killer— some punk who called himself La Rata, The Rat, started to deface Barney's suburban canvases. Right next to Barney's La Cucaracha, a large black rat suddenly appeared. It was twice the size of Barney's cockroach, its huge jaws about to munch on Barney's poor unsuspecting pest. What made the violation worse was that La Rata was not only a damn good artist but kids liked his sense of humor, the town's newspaper running a headline that read COCKROACH EATEN BY RAT. When even Barney found himself laughing at the paper's comic description of La Rata's graffiti, he knew something had to be done.

That's why, on the night of that unexpected gunshot, he was looking at hundreds of fonts and scouring the Internet for images of cockroaches.

Unfortunately, he couldn't find a depiction of a cockroach that was really shocking, something that would make La Rata's rat look like a first-grade art project. So he just began to doodle, starting with a bug whose head and belly faced the viewer. He penciled in big blue eyes that were trapped in oversize black tortoiseshell glasses. Then he added some wavy black hair, a somewhat demonic smile, and a large nose, made more conspicuous by an M&M-sized bump on its bridge.

By the time he was done, the insect looked like a cross between a computer geek and a prizefighter, with a pissed-off expression that Barney exaggerated by painting tiny beads of blood dripping from its teeth.

He scrutinized his new creation, then walked to the window. Sirens were wailing and he hoped the cops had finally caught La Rata. Not seeing anything outside, he returned to his drawing. Truth be told, this revised La Cucaracha creeped him out, reminding him that there were nooks and crannies in the basement of his unconscious that shouldn't be visited. And yet there was something eerily familiar about this new, improved cockroach.

What was it?

"Jesus," he said out loud, though Barney was an avowed atheist.

What Barney saw was himself: his big bug eyes and black glasses, his slightly deformed nose (though a few girls thought it was cute).

It was then that La Cucaracha became La Cucaracha Humana.

The Human Cockroach.

That night, in spite of the shot and sirens, at about 2 a.m., after three Red Bulls, he snuck out of the house and painted his creation next to where La Rata's first rat had appeared. Underneath it he wrote La Cucaracha Humana in a spooky font he stole from a New York City gangbanger: large red letters that seemed to melt like warm wax before his eyes.

"Take that, you asshole," he said, finishing up his last brushstroke and nervously glancing around.

He didn't sleep well that night, either because of the Red Bulls or because of the anxiety hangover from constantly looking over his shoulder for cop cars. About every half hour he woke to the sensation of creepy-crawly things feasting on his body. He flipped on a light and examined his skinny white torso. He even shook out his comforter and was surprised that no six-legged creatures tumbled onto the floor.

The next day he expected everyone to be talking about La Cucaracha Humana, but no one mentioned it. How could they have missed it on their way to school? None of it made sense until he heard, along with everyone else, that a classmate, Alex Youngblood, had been gunned down on the bike path, which explained the shot he'd heard the night before. In Barney's town, Martians landing and impregnating able-bodied sixteen-year-old girls would've have been less upsetting than a murder like this, even though most kids hadn't liked Alex. He was a bully and what Barney called a "downsized person." Barney figured that he'd probably slept with the wrong girl this time and the outraged dad had taken him out, though most kids thought wangstas from Riverside jumped him and things had gotten out of hand.

Whatever, it was hard for Barney to care much about it, since Alex and the other cool kids were as unreal to him as characters in a book or a movie. Still, a few nights later he decided to go to an outdoor vigil for Alex, thinking that if he were around a large group of kids, his La Cucaracha Humana might finally come up. But everyone just stood around holding lit candles and pretending they were best friends with Alex. By the time the vigil ended, Barney hoped that Alex was put to rest for good and that La Cucaracha Humana might rise from his ashes. For that to happen, though, he knew he'd have to paint a few more giant cockroaches around town.

So the next night he gathered his paint and brushes and threaded his way through a wooded path that led to the public library. Two weeks ago, after whitewashing a No LITTERING sign that had been planted between the library and a playground, La Rata had painted an image of his nasty rodent on it. The next morning a few toddlers got freaked out by the giant rat as they stumbled innocently toward a jungle gym. Outraged parents quickly yanked the sign from the ground and tossed it into the woods. Barney planned to find the sign, leave his mark next to La Rata, and then replant the sign near a bus stop on Route 114, the main drag that ran in front of the town hall. That way, as early-morning commuters drove by, they'd be greeted by La Cucaracha Humana about to nibble on La Rata's ugly snout.

"Let's see what the paper'll say about that," Barney mumbled, as he made his way through the woods. It was warmer than usual, with a full moon just beginning to lose its perfect shape. Considering what had happened to Alex, he shouldn't have been wandering alone in the woods at night, but, as he surmised, that shooting had occurred on the other side of town.

Right before he reached the library he heard laughter. He slowed his pace, then crouched behind a nearby tree. From there he saw someone by a tall concrete backstop the town had constructed so that kids could practice lacrosse. The intruder was talking to himself, splashing and spreading big globs of white paint on the wall with a large house-painting brush.

Barney decided to let him finish priming the wall and then burst in before the kid could start painting a new La Rata. It was a good plan until the kid turned and said, "I can hear you, La Cucaracha. I know you're there. Barney Roth, right?"

It was Tyler Whitney.

"Can't say I expected this," Barney said, after stepping out from the shadows.

Tyler laughed. He was a big guy, a jock, though pretty smart and popular, and as far as Barney remembered, he wasn't a jerk like most of his friends.

"What I meant was …"

"What you meant was that you didn't think someone like me could draw."

"How did you know it was me?" Barney asked.

Tyler stood there, paint dripping from his brush. "I knew we'd eventually cross paths," he said, "and your paint-supply bag gave you away."

"It's a satchel."

97

Tyler laughed again. Barney had been laughed at by jocks before, but not by one who was smart, a damn good artist, and infuriatingly good-looking, even with his buzz cut. It was like being a half-starved, bald Buddhist monk and finding out that Brad Pitt was into meditation and did it better than you.

"So what happens now?" Barney said. "We duel to the death with our brushes?"

Tyler seemed to be considering that possibility. "A better question is, Do we have to be enemies? I mean, we're doing the same thing, right?"

"In a way, but your rat was very aggressive, dude. He wanted to eat my La Cucaracha."

"It was a joke."

"Yeah, and everyone got it."

"I'm surprised you're pissed. I mean, you're always busting kids at school, so I thought you'd appreciate an epic battle between La Rata and La Cucaracha."

"How did you know La Cucaracha was mine?" Barney asked. "Not even my friends know that."

"One hint, Barney. If you wanna keep something like that secret, don't always be scribbling on an artist's pad when the teacher's back is turned. I mean, I draw, so I noticed."

"So when did you decide to draw La Rata?"

"When I saw La Cucaracha on the dumpster at the Little League field. A stroke of genius, dude."

"Thanks."

"No, really, you're good."

Barney's head was spinning. He was flattered but also confused by where the flattery was coming from. "Better watch what you say, dude," he said. "You don't want your friends to hear you."

"Hey, they're not all assholes," Tyler said. "You really gotta lose that jocks-versus-geeks stuff. You're the guys who think you're smarter than everyone."

"I dunno, everyone thinks La Rata is a fucking genius, but that's because they haven't seen this." Barney reached into his satchel and took out his sketch of La Cucaracha Humana. He handed it to Tyler, who burst into laughter.

"You won't be too anonymous after kids see this," Tyler said, then paused thoughtfully before adding, "Don't you think every La Cucaracha Humana deserves a La Rata Humana?"

And so Barney watched as Tyler let his house-painting brush drop to the ground, grabbed a sketchpad from his supply bag, and began working on a large rat that, as promised, looked a little like Tyler Whitney. As Tyler drew, Barney noticed a two-inch slash over his left eyebrow. "How did you get that scar? Football?"

Tyler continued to scratch away as he spoke. "No, I fell down the basement stairs when I was about three."

"You gotta include that," Barney said, pleased when Tyler not only sketched the scar but enlarged and transformed it by adding a Frankenstein cross-stitch. When he was finished, Barney could only offer admiration. "Very cool," he said.

A smile of satisfaction spread over Tyler's face. "Believe it or not, Barney, that means something to me."

Barney waited for an obligatory chest bump that never arrived, though he and Tyler did decide to collaborate on a new project. It would've been easier to use the concrete backstop as their canvas, but the paint Tyler had spread earlier hadn't dried, so they decided on the white concrete back wall of Froyo, a local yogurt place. During the day, the wall was clearly visible to anyone biking, walking, or jogging on the bike path, which was about half the people in their town.

It took Barney and Tyler about ten minutes to reach Froyo, where they unpacked their paint and brushes and worked feverishly on their collaboration, their arms flailing like two manic orchestra conductors. They painted separately and together, moonlight casting their shadows against the wall, so that it appeared that four people instead of two were at work. Their vermin acquired more and more personality as human features were added and movements suggested. The mural now had a narrative, because next to La Cucaracha Humana and La Rata Humana, Barney and Tyler had drawn a few naked, terrified kids—their mouths frozen in screams—fleeing from two creepy predators about to feast on their pale teenage asses. It had been Barney's idea to make them naked.

When they finished, they collapsed at the base of a nearby tree.

"You think the cops will figure out who did it?" Tyler asked.

"You care?" Barney replied.

"In a way, yeah. Last year the Providence cops put a graffiti artist in jail. They wanted to make an example of him."

"That won't happen here," Barney said as he admired the mural, realizing that he and Tyler would never be able to do something so cool again. "Might be best to put La Cucaracha Humana and La Rata Humana to rest after tonight," he said. "We made our point. People will be pissed off for a few days, then go back to living with their heads up their asses."

Tyler grudgingly agreed, and they gathered their supplies and headed toward the bike path.

"Which way?" Tyler said.

Barney pointed toward Echo Pond.

"Me, too," Tyler said.

It didn't take long until they reached a faintly lit stretch of the path. They walked about a quarter of a mile before being surprised by a kid sitting on a huge boulder that faced the pond.

"Just keep moving," Tyler whispered.

Just as they were about to pass the kid, he turned and said, "Hey, what's all the whispering about?" He stood and walked toward them, his hands stuffed in the rear pockets of his jeans. He was big, with long shaggy dark hair that fell over his shoulders like clumps of wet seaweed. He wore dark shorts, a black Hurley T-shirt, and beat-up black Vans. He was smiling as if he knew something they didn't.

At least it was two to one, Barney thought.

"I don't like whispering," the kid said.

Barney had never been in this situation before. His heart was racing, and his feet seemed frozen to the ground. In contrast, Tyler was calm. "We're cool here," Tyler said to the kid. "So you can go back to whatever the fuck you were doing."

Barney waited for the kid to respond, but a different voice came from somewhere behind them. "Yeah, Eddie," the voice said, "go back to whatever the fuck you were doing."

When Barney and Tyler turned, four kids emerged from the woods, laughing and shoving each other.

The kid who spoke was short but muscled, his white T-shirt fitting like a second skin. He flashed an evil grin that he'd probably spent most of high school perfecting in his bathroom mirror. Barney's head was spinning so fast he couldn't focus on the other three kids. "That's no way to talk to Eddie," the short kid said.

Tyler smiled and let his supply bag fall to the ground.

"Why the fuck do you guys have paint all over you?" the short kid asked.

"We were working on a mural," Barney said.

"A what?"

"It's like a painting."

"Just drop it, Barney," Tyler said. "He's not interested."

But Barney was nervous, and when he got that way he jabbered. "You the guys who killed Alex?"

"Who's Alex?" the kid said.

"He's talking about the punk who got capped a few nights ago, Paulie," the kid named Eddie said.

"No way," Paulie said. "We don't do that shit. We're Riverside boys."

"We know where you're from," Tyler said, the expression on his face never changing.

"You play football?" Paulie asked. "Shit, look at the size of his neck. I used to play, but the coach had too many rules." Then he surprised everyone by stepping into Tyler's space and jabbing both palms into his chest. "You know," he said, "for a quarter, we might just let you guys go." He shoved Tyler again, this time harder.

And that's when Tyler struck back.

Barney hoped that Tyler would knock the guy out, so they could run to the closest house for help. But instead, something extraordinary happened. Well, two things, really, and to understand them you had to know another of Barney's secrets.

Just this year Barney had become a Bruce Lee freak, his favorite movie being *Enter the Dragon*, his favorite scene the one where Lee fights his arch-rival's bodyguard. Lee prances around like a prizefighter

101

on speed while the bodyguard tries to stab him with a broken bottle, which, in the world of martial arts, is a very uncool thing to do. In response, Lee knocks the guy down with an acrobatic kick to the jaw, leaps about three feet into the air, then comes down on the guy's throat, apparently crushing his windpipe. The camera never shows the maiming. Instead, it focuses on Lee's face as he lets out a creepy banshee wail.

Barney must've have practiced that fight scene a few hundred times on his father's punching bag, which hung from a thick metal hook in his basement. He may have been tall and skinny, but he had developed one powerful kick, which, much to his surprise, he unleashed into the solar plexus of an unsuspecting Paulie, who went down in a heap. Then he went into his Bruce Lee jig before taking out another guy with a kick to the groin, while Tyler and Eddie wrestled each other to the ground. All of this would've have been heroic, the stuff kids would've talked about for a very long time, but even Bruce Lee moves weren't going to offset the odds.

And that's when the second extraordinary thing happened.

Out of nowhere a huge kid appeared, swinging a tree limb the size of a baseball bat. Barney heard a few oofs and ughs before Paulie and his gang scrambled away, grasping various parts of their bodies. The huge kid, with his back to Barney and still holding the branch, laughed and taunted the punks as they ran off. Then he turned and faced Barney and Tyler, saying, "If it ain't my homeboy, Tyler."

Tyler wiped blood from the side of his mouth and managed a smile. "Adam," he said. "Why aren't I surprised?"

Barney knew this Adam well. In fact, he had recently contacted him when a friend of his had needed help. Adam was a loner, a football player, a kid no one messed with, who looked like he'd been constructed from blocks of flesh, all lines and angles. It was rumored that he and a few other demented guys had started a hit squad called Muscle, and for a price they'd intimidate just about anyone, which was why Barney had spoken with him.

"Do we have to pay for this?" Tyler said.

"Nah, this is for the team." He sized up Barney, then turned to

Tyler. "You guys lovers?"

"Don't push it, Adam," Tyler said.

"Well, it's pretty late to be wandering around, especially with a geek."

"Fuck you," Barney said, the adrenaline talking for him.

"Normally," Adam said, "I'd shove this branch up your ass for saying that, but you were an impressive little prick in that fight. What was that squeal about? You sounded like your balls were on fire."

"It's from *Enter the Dragon*. It's a Bruce Lee movie," Barney said.

"You mean the Chink?"

"Yeah," Barney said, shaking his head in disgust. "The Chink."

"You making fun of me?"

"Yeah, I guess I am," Barney said, surprising himself again with his bravado.

Tyler seemed annoyed by their banter. He grabbed his supply bag and slung it over his shoulder. "Why did you wait so long, Adam?" he said. "We could've gotten our asses kicked."

Adam smiled, a thick crease disfiguring his forehead. "I wanted to see how you'd do first."

Barney had calmed down by now, though the rush of his first fight since second grade (he'd lost that one) had wasted him, and he felt, strangely, like crying. He wondered how guys like Adam did this all the time, and he longed for a few peaceful moments with his sketchpad.

"You want me to chill with you guys for a while?" Adam said. "Those wangstas might come back."

"We'll be okay," Tyler said.

"How about you, Roth? You okay?"

"Fucking peachy," Barney said. "And thanks for letting us almost get killed."

"You know, Roth," Adam said, "the problem with you geeks is that you don't know when to shut up. That's why you guys've been beat on since kindygarten."

"Kindygarten?"

"Let it go, Barney," Tyler said.

And for once Barney did, watching silently as Adam dropped

his club and faded into the woods like some yet-to-be-discovered Sasquatch.

After Adam left, he and Tyler sat on the bike path. Barney traced the line painted down the middle of the pavement, while Tyler pulled out a pack of gum and offered him a stick. "That was some weird shit you did tonight," Tyler said. "I mean, I gotta watch that movie."

"Can I ask you something, Tyler?" he said.

"Yeah, sure."

"Why didn't we just give the kid a quarter? Maybe he would've left."

"You've got a lot to learn about assholes, Barney," Tyler said. Then he stood up and walked toward the boulder Eddie had earlier occupied, leaning his ass against it. "Come on, there's room for two."

"You sure no one will think we're lovers?"

"You're a funny guy, Barney. After school ends, we should hang out, maybe have a few beers to toast the beginning and end of La Cucaracha Humana and La Rata Humana."

Barney agreed, and then they sat silently next to each other, staring out across Echo Pond, which the moon had transformed into a giant watery mirror. After a few minutes Barney broke the silence. "I gotta go, Tyler."

"Yeah," Tyler said. "Probably a good idea."

So they grabbed their supply bags and walked for about a half mile before splitting off—Tyler toward the country club, Barney toward his middle-class neighborhood.

Barney reached his house way after his curfew. He wedged open the screen on the basement window and slid through its opening. Then he climbed the stairs into the kitchen, poured a glass of orange juice, and sat at the kitchen table in semi-darkness until a light came on. Before him stood his father in nothing but plain white boxer shorts. He looked half asleep, his hair tousled, the bags under his eyes fatter and darker than usual, gray hairs sprouting from his ears and nose. Barney felt a twinge of pity for his mother having this hairy, paunchy man for a bedmate, and he hoped there wasn't any truth to the saying "Like father, like son."

"What're you doing up, Barn?" his father mumbled, wiping

something crusty from his right eye.

"Couldn't sleep, Dad," Barney said.

"Why're you dressed?"

"Never got undressed."

"Well, clean up after yourself so your mom doesn't have a shit conniption."

"Sure, Dad, just go back to your beauty sleep."

His father laughed. "You're a card, Barney."

"That's the rumor."

Fifteen minutes later Barney was stretched out on his bed, staring up at a ceiling fan that spun so fast he couldn't distinguish the blades.

He felt anxious, so he sat up, grabbed his sketchpad from the bed stand, and started to draw. Human figures tramping down the bike path materialized before his eyes. They were Paulie and his friends, frozen in exaggerated gangsta walks. Behind them, a massive serpentine head appeared, its tongue flicking between two menacing fangs, its long, thick body lagging behind like a piece of severed intestine.

"La Cobra Humana," Barney said, imagining Tyler howling at the sketch the next day at school. And at that thought, he felt a hard-on poking its way through the open fly of his boxer shorts.

"What the fuck?" was about all he could say.

THE SAINT

With the Fourth of July only a few weeks away, Missy Rogers was sure the sound was fireworks. Her brother Eric had almost blown off his thumb with an M-80 when he was fourteen, and it sounded like that, except the boom from the M-80 had left her ears ringing for an hour, while this explosion came and went like momentary thunder. Her house was only a short walk from the bike path that bordered Echo Pond, and from her window she could see the moon's reflection on the calm water—a stark contrast to the blast. But then her bedroom door flew open. Silhouetted by a hall light, Eric was standing in the threshold wearing nothing but boxer shorts.

"What was that?"

"Why don't you put on some clothes?" she said.

"Why don't you answer my question?" he responded, brushing his dark hair back over his shoulders with both hands.

Missy was used to Eric's attitude. He'd always been difficult, acting up in school or at summer camp, and he'd gotten worse since their brother Ethan had died. It was as if Ethan's death proved to Eric, once and for all, that the world sucked, which in turn gave him permission to act out more than he had before.

"I can't answer your question because I don't know what that noise was," Missy said.

"Sounded like a gunshot. Maybe Mom finally blew her brains out."

"That's not funny."

"I'm not trying to be funny. By the way, her door's open, and she's not there."

A wave of panic swept over Missy. She pushed past Eric and ran toward their mother's bedroom. When she got there she turned on the light, only to discover an unmade bed, so she checked the bathroom and then downstairs. She even went into the garage, imagining her mother hunched over the steering wheel, weeping over old photos of Ethan while exhaust fumes poisoned her lungs.

Eric was right behind her. "Want me to call Dad? That's what you're thinking, right?"

Missy barely heard him. She was trying to form a plan. "I hope she's not wandering again. It's those sleeping pills. She goes off and doesn't remember where she went or what she did."

"They aren't bad," Eric said, wanting Missy to know he'd been stealing his mother's meds.

"Just get dressed, will you?" she said before going back upstairs, this time passing Ethan's room. Nothing inside had been touched since he died, and her mother had forbidden them to enter the room. She'd even had a new doorknob with a lock installed, and only she had the key. Missy jiggled the doorknob, then knocked a few times.

"You expecting Ethan to open it?" Eric said from behind her. She saw that he had thrown on a pair of jeans and a T-shirt.

"Why do you have to be so mean?" Missy said.

"I can get in if you want."

"How can you do that?"

He smiled and disappeared for a moment, then returned with a key and a small hammer.

"I thought only Mom had a key to that door," she said.

"She does. This is a bump key."

"A what?"

"A bump key." He fitted the key into the lock and tapped it with the hammer. Then he turned the knob and pushed the door open.

"How did you do that?"

"Sometimes you need to get into places."

"Like that hardware store?"

"That was never proved."

Actually, it was until Missy's father made the problem go away.

Eric opened the door, then lurked behind as Missy went inside. As she'd expected, her mother was curled up on the bottom mattress of Ethan's bunk bed. Her head was on a pillow from which the stem of a feather protruded. Fearing it might harm her, Missy plucked the feather and placed it on a nightstand.

"I used to sleep right where Mom is," Eric said. "Ethan was worried that if I got on top, the bed would crash down on him. He had my weight measured in kilos, you know that?"

Missy went to comfort him, but he pulled back.

"I don't need anyone's help. It's like Dad said, 'Why couldn't it have been Eric instead of Ethan?'"

"He was drunk that night," Missy protested, "and you were goading him. And he didn't say it like that or know you could hear him."

"Just don't bother me tonight if anything else happens," he said. "I'm not the one who's The Saint."

"Don't you want to help Mom?"

He pointed to a bottle of wine on the bed stand. "She has all the help she needs," he said, as he turned and headed for the door.

Missy hated being called The Saint. It wasn't her fault she liked helping people. She never understood why other kids complained about delivering clothes to the homeless or serving meals at the senior center. She wondered if her mother was right, that maybe there was an altruism gene. Some people had it, some didn't. But how could you just live for yourself?

Missy picked up the wine bottle and saw that it was empty. She shifted her gaze to her mother, who was clutching a multicolored comforter she'd knitted for Ethan when he was two. She was always so stylish and upbeat, but then Ethan got sick, and she seemed to take on his cancer. Missy understood how that could happen because, in a way, that's what she was doing—taking on her mother's grief in an attempt to lead her back to the living, though, unlike her mother, she was determined not to let that grief destroy her.

She set down the wine bottle and pulled on a chain hanging from the socket of a nearby lamp. More light filled the room. On the walls were posters of famous athletes and one of the periodic table. Ethan had always been obsessed with chemistry and had spent his last year knowing exactly what chemicals were battling his disease. He treated his illness like a school project he had to write a paper on.

To Missy, the room still smelled of sickness, and now wine. She opened a window and a slight breeze stirred the drapes. She gently nudged her mother to consciousness, then sat next to her.

"What? What?" her mother said.

"You're in Ethan's room, Mom. I was worried about you."

She was groggy but seemed able to process Missy's words. Then she spoke again, her voice sounding like the faint echo of her real voice. "You shouldn't be here, Missy. Sometimes I hear him moving. I don't want to scare him away." She looked at the open window. "You have to close that or we'll lose his smell, and then he'll be gone for good."

Missy stroked her mother's hair. "Ethan would've wanted it open," she said. "You know how much he loved nature."

Her mother smiled and gripped the comforter, inhaling its smell.

"Let's get you to bed, okay?" Missy said.

Her mother stood, then stumbled, almost falling down. Missy steadied her and led her to the door.

"Wait," her mother said, breaking free. She leaned over the bed and carefully spread the comforter, as if tucking someone in. She lingered there until Missy joined her. In the hallway Eric was waiting. Her mother moved toward him and grabbed his hand, then Missy's. "My two babies," she said. "I was always so lucky."

Eric sighed. "Yeah, Mom, you're really blessed."

"Yes, blessed is the word."

Missy glared at Eric.

"She won't even remember the conversation tomorrow," Eric said.

After Missy got her mother undressed and settled in her own room, her mother asked for her rosary and holy card of Saint Jude. The card, given to her mother by Missy's grandmother, was over forty years old, faded and wrinkled. Saint Jude was the patron saint of hopeless cases, and Missy couldn't understand why anyone would give a card like that to someone they loved.

Missy's mother grasped the cross in her palm and wrapped the beads around her wrist. Missy knew what was coming next. She sat quietly while her mother, with eyes closed, began: "Oh glorious apostle Saint Jude, faithful servant and friend of Jesus, the name of the traitor who delivered thy beloved Master into the hands of His enemies has caused thee to be forgotten by many, but the Church honors and invokes thee universally as the patron of hopeless cases—of things despaired of. Pray for me who am so miserable; make use, I implore thee, of that particular privilege accorded thee of bringing visible and speedy help where help is almost despaired of ..."

As she neared the end of the prayer, her words became almost a whisper, and shortly after her final Amen she drifted off to sleep.

Ten minutes later Missy found herself in the kitchen with Eric, who was pouring Lucky Charms into a bowl. He leaned against a counter, picking at the snack, his upper lip dusted with some crumbs. "Yet another Rogers family drama," he said.

"You've certainly had your own," Missy said.

"It just pisses me off how they've fallen apart."

"It's called mourning."

"But look at you. You go right on saving the world, smiling like some drugged chimpanzee."

"I'm trying to honor Ethan's life."

"You're just a misery junkie."

"That's hurtful, Eric."

"What's hurtful is watching Mom collapse while Dad's doing ... what? Do you even know where he is?"

In fact, Missy often did. "I'm going for a walk," she said.

"Probably not a good idea after that shot."

"How do you know it was a shot?"

"What else could it be?" he said, before walking away.

Missy shelved the box of cereal, then left the kitchen, heading for the front door. Outside, the night was full with the sound of crickets and the errant flights of June bugs, which had come early that year. From the street, Missy looked up at Ethan's room. The window was still open, and off to the right were brief on-and-off flashes like tiny

Christmas lights. Fireflies, Missy thought, though she'd never seen that many so close together or so high in the air.

She kept to the sidewalk, knowing where she was going. About halfway there, she heard sirens, and then two police cars sped by with their lights flashing. She turned, relieved when they veered off away from her house. She was just about to reach a main road heading toward the small strip mall in town when she saw a figure coming toward her—a short boy with both hands stuffed in his pockets. She thought about the shot and the police cars but continued on, keeping her eyes down. When she and the figure met under a streetlight, she looked up, glad to see Robert Hammersmith, a boy she shared a few classes with.

"Hi," he said. "Missy, right?"

"Hi, Robert."

"Math and history, right?"

"Yeah."

He seemed nervous as he ran his hand through his curly black hair. She noticed a red splotch above his left cheek. He saw her staring at it and gently rubbed the spot. "It's a long story," he said, then added, "Something pretty weird just happened on the bicycle path. The cops said someone got shot. Maybe you shouldn't be out."

"They must've made a mistake," Missy said.

"Still ..."

"I'll be okay," she said. "I'm almost where I need to be." Missy had never noticed Robert's eyes before, very large and kind.

"But really, I'll walk with you if you want. I mean, until you get there."

"Thanks, but I'm fine."

"I wasn't trying to hit on you or anything," he said. "It just seemed like the right thing to say."

"It was, Robert. I appreciate it."

"Well, okay then," he said, and headed in the other direction.

Missy walked for twenty or thirty yards before turning to see if he was still in sight. At the same time, Robert must've turned, because they were staring at each other. He raised his hand and waved, and so did she before resuming her journey.

It took only fifteen minutes to reach Pizzico, a pricey Italian restaurant in town. Through the windows Missy could see people eating in the air-conditioned half of the dining room and others munching on appetizers at small outside tables that were draped with white linen. The other half of the indoor restaurant had a fancy bar area with large windows that could be slid open during the summer, as they were then. She stood in the parking lot, the din of conversation penetrating the night. About twenty people sat at the long bar, her father being one of them. His sports coat was hanging from the back of his chair and his tie was loosened.

Missy moved closer.

Her father was with a blond woman who couldn't have been more than thirty. His left hand was resting on her knee. The woman had a round face and a pleasant smile. She was very animated, laughing at whatever her father was saying. It was hard to think he could make anyone laugh anymore, but then she remembered how often he had made jokes before Ethan died. Involuntarily, she moved toward the window until she was a few feet from a young couple eating a gourmet pizza at one of the outside tables. They looked startled, probably wondering who this intruder was.

It was then that the pretty woman spotted Missy and stopped laughing, looking inquisitively at her. Her father's eyes followed the woman's glance until he too saw Missy. He set down his glass and stepped down from his barstool, moving toward the door. Embarrassed, Missy tried to jog away, but he caught up to her in the parking lot and grabbed her by the arm, though not forcefully.

"Is something wrong?"

Missy was determined not to cry. "I was just worried, and I know you like this place."

Her father was tall and handsome, with striking blue eyes and thick blond hair that was long and shaggy enough to make him look rugged. He pointed toward the restaurant. "I don't want you to get the wrong idea. She works at the bank. I'll introduce you if you want."

"No," was all she said.

"Well, at least wait for me, okay? I just need to get my jacket."

She watched as he returned to the restaurant. He said a few words to the pretty woman and left some money on the bar. Missy tried to see the woman's face. Did she look concerned? Annoyed? Mad? Her father draped his sports coat over his arm, gently touched the woman's arm, and left.

The drive home was quiet until Missy said, "Mom's been going into Ethan's room."

"I know," her father said, his eyes fixed on the road.

"Why didn't you tell me?"

"For what purpose?"

"It might help me to understand."

Her father pulled over, letting the car idle. "There's nothing to understand," he said. "We've lost your mother for now. I've tried everything. I really have."

"Is that woman your girlfriend?" she said.

He shifted his eyes from the road to Missy. "No, just a friend. Am I betraying your mother by laughing once in a while? You think I like sleeping in the spare room, or watching her do odd things like having that lock installed on Ethan's door?"

"I see changes in her," Missy said. "I really do." That wasn't true, but she felt she might will it to be true if she tried hard enough.

Her father smiled. "You're an amazing girl."

"Kids make fun of me. They call me The Saint."

"People can be very nasty. There's not much for them to do but to gossip and assign people roles they don't want. Many of them enjoy it when Eric goes off and embarrasses us, and I know your mother's friends think I've abandoned her."

"You haven't, though, have you?"

"Of course not."

"Then talk to her when we get home. I swear, I saw a glimmer of the old Mom tonight. I felt like I was getting through to her."

"I'll try," he said.

"And will you talk to Eric, too?"

"You can't talk to someone if he's not listening, and that has nothing to do with Ethan's death."

"But he mentioned that comment again tonight."

"What comment?"

"When you wished it had been him instead of Ethan."

"That was after he was arrested," he said. "It was a terrible thing to say, and I apologized, but it's always been your brother's modus operandi to push you until you say something horrible, so he can be a victim."

"Will you talk to him anyway?"

Her father seemed exasperated by her request. "I'll try, Missy."

She leaned over and kissed him on his cheek, and then her father pulled away from the curb. A few blocks from their house red lights flashed somewhere in the vicinity of the pond.

"I wonder what that's about," he said.

Missy didn't mention what Robert Hammersmith had told her. For now, she was tired of being The Saint. So many people to save, so many fires to light or put out.

* * *

Missy had been friends with Alex Youngblood in grammar school but hadn't hung out with him much since. What was nervous energy in him as a middle schooler seemed to morph into meanness as a teenager. Still, she was saddened to learn that the noise she had heard that night was indeed a gunshot and that its victim was Alex. Kids offered the police many reasons for the shooting. Alex had always bragged about being rich, so maybe he was carrying a wad of money with him that night. Or maybe he was shot by a jealous boyfriend, since Alex was always trying to pick up girls. The way he chose to live was foreign to Missy, but she knew better than anyone that any death, especially if it was sudden, was a tragedy.

But if that were true, why did kids seem more curious than sad? Some even made jokes. The only person who broke down was a girl named Maura, a girl Alex had been dating. Missy was in the hallway when Maura collapsed onto the floor near Alex's locker. Everyone froze for a few seconds, except for two girls who giggled before walking away.

For some reason, that strange reaction seemed to normalize the scene, and everyone went back to their business, probably hoping that when they looked again Maura would be gone.

But Missy stayed. She knelt beside Maura and gathered the books Maura had dropped. "Are you okay?" she asked.

"I'm fine," Maura said, trying to compose herself.

She certainly didn't seem fine. Her clothes were wrinkled, and she looked like she hadn't had much sleep. Missy wanted to mention Alex but felt the timing was wrong. The bell for the next class sounded, and Maura said, "You're going to be late."

"It's okay," Missy said, still helping Maura to get organized. "Maybe you should go home. No one would blame you."

"Thanks, but I'd feel better if you just went to class," Maura said, with a smile that was so forced it appeared crooked.

That's when the assistant principal, Ms. Stang, appeared in the hallway. She was a heavy woman with big blue eyes and rouged chubby cheeks. She always wore black pantsuits and black pointy shoes, and she was never seen without a ruler in her hand, which made her intimidating.

"What's this?" she asked, her expression a mixture of pleasure and annoyance, though she changed abruptly upon seeing Missy. "Can you tell me why we're all standing in the hall, Missy, while classes are in session? You're not someone I'd expect to be in this position."

"I got dizzy and kind of passed out," Missy said, "and Maura hung around to help."

Ms. Stang scratched her head with the ruler, moving her lips and jaw as if chewing on this story. "Well then, let's get you down to the nurse, and you," she said, looking at Maura, "go to class and tell your teachers I'll explain your tardiness later."

Maura nodded, and when Ms. Stang turned her back, Maura mouthed, "Thank you."

* * *

Missy was surprised when she didn't see Maura at Alex's vigil. In fact, half of the kids she had expected were absent, and she was beginning

116

to regret organizing the event. At the time it seemed like the right thing to do. After she had freed herself from the school nurse, she waited for normal reactions to the shooting, any expression of loss or sadness, but all anyone cared about was themselves. "Is the town safe anymore?" "Are my parents going to make stricter curfews?" "Will we be able to throw parties or get stoned in the cemetery with cops prowling all over the place?"

It was as if kids were mad at Alex for getting shot, messing up the last few weeks before their senior year ended.

Missy thought a vigil might be a good antidote to this insensitivity, but, ironically, the gathering was beginning to resemble a poorly planned high school dance. She wished she had gotten an oversize picture of Alex made and displayed on an easel to remind kids of why they were there. But she hadn't had much time to coordinate the event, and if she had waited a week or two, no one would've cared.

But she did have a schedule for the vigil printed up:

1) Gathering at 8:30 p.m.
2) Handing out and lighting of candles at 8:45 p.m.
3) A moment of silence.

What Missy hadn't expected were people arriving early, especially the jocks. They had been drinking and were now smoking pot, and Missy feared what would happen if the police showed up.

What surprised her even more was the presence of kids Alex didn't even like. There was the boy Robert, whom she'd passed on the street a few nights ago. He was with a number of his friends, who were into things like skateboarding and comic book collecting—not hobbies Alex would've cared about. One tall, gangly kid named Barney was the oddest of them all. Missy was convinced he had Tourette's Syndrome because he made strange comments at the weirdest times. But he was funny, if you liked that kind of humor. Missy started to hand out candles until one of the jocks, Campbell McVeigh, said, "What are we supposed to do with these?"

"Why don't you use it like a rectal thermometer," another jock said.

"Or a dildo," Campbell added, laughing.

"Not very nice," Missy said to Campbell.

"Hey, I just asked a question," Campbell said.

"And it was a stupid one," the kid named Barney suddenly blurted out. He was standing with his friends ten feet away.

From the look on Campbell's face, it appeared that a fight might break out until the boy named Robert sidled away from his friends and approached Missy. "You need any help?" he asked, pointing to the candles.

"What's *this* about?" Campbell snarled. He said something about Robert looking like a hobbit, then finished with, "You're a little bit out of your league, Maurice."

"His name's Robert," Missy said.

"He knows my name," Robert said.

"That I do," Campbell admitted, "but you still haven't told me what I'm supposed to do with this candle."

"It's what scientists give to monkeys," the boy named Barney said.

"What?"

"You know, an object to keep them from playing with their feces."

Missy laughed in spite of herself, while the boy named Robert shook his head and said, "Cool it, Barney."

"Just trying to have your back," Barney said.

"My back's fine," Robert said.

"Your back's tiny and looks like a girl's," Campbell said, which made the other jocks roll on the ground with laughter.

Missy could see Robert wince. "Thanks, Robert," she said, handing him some candles and flyers. Then she tugged on the hem of his T-shirt, hoping to steer him away from the jocks.

"Just ignore them," she said.

"Campbell and I have a history," Robert said, which made Missy remember the bruise she'd seen on his face a few nights before.

Robert followed her until all the candles had been handed out and lit. Then everyone, even the jocks, observed a moment of silence.

Things started to unravel a bit after that. It was like different pockets of people didn't want to leave or had forgotten why they'd come, so Missy asked Robert to help her carry the leftover flyers and candles to her car. Then she said, "Would you mind going for a walk?"

Robert looked surprised. "Where?"

"Just down to the beach. I need to clear my head."

"Sure," he said. "But I have to text Barney. He's my ride."

"I can drive you home," Missy said.

"Really?"

"Absolutely."

After Robert checked in with his friend, Missy led him toward the beach. "I'm afraid this vigil's been a bit of a failure," she said.

"That's not your fault," Robert said.

They walked on silently for a while. Then Missy asked, "Why did you come tonight? You weren't friends with Alex."

"I'm not really sure," he said.

Soon they reached the beach, which was no more than a thirty-yard-wide ribbon of soft sand separating Narragansett Bay from a row of huge houses along the coast. Once Alex's house was out of sight, Missy sat down on the sand. She waited for Robert to join her, but he remained standing, fidgeting.

"You going to sit?"

"Sure," he said, settling in next to her.

"Thanks," she said.

"For what?"

"For being here. At the vigil I was thinking that even after four years, there're so many kids I don't know. Our school is too big."

"Big is good. You can be anonymous."

"But if you're anonymous, you don't get anything done or help anyone."

Robert seemed surprised by her comment.

"I meant, like taking chances," she added. She watched his face, worried she had offended him. She slid closer to him and grabbed his hand, while he continued to look straight ahead. "You okay?"

"It's not like I've never been with a girl before."

"We can leave if you want to."

"No, this is nice. I just didn't expect to be sitting on the beach and holding hands with Missy Rogers tonight. I mean, you're part of Alex's crew."

"Not really. He just belonged to my country club."

Missy scanned the beach. The bay was calm, as if the tide couldn't decide whether to ebb or flow. She was tired and disappointed by how the vigil had turned out, but sitting next to Robert, she felt relaxed. He didn't seem to need or want anything from her. She leaned over and pecked him on the cheek, and when he turned, she started to kiss him. He seemed startled at first, but then returned the kiss, both of them losing their balance and falling onto their backs. They laughed and continued to lie there, sometimes kissing, sometimes staring up at the full moon, which, to Missy, seemed so full of promise, so full of hope.

VIGIL

Alex Youngblood was as surprised as anyone that someone was holding a vigil for him. He didn't know how he felt about it, partly because he hadn't felt anything since the bullet blew a hole through his heart. What were the chances that Maura would've had the nerve to pull that trigger as he walked away? At first he thought she'd thrown something—a rock, maybe—that knocked the wind out of him, but try as he might, he couldn't catch his breath, and then, bit by bit, he felt what had to be his soul slipping away into the night, death's slow gnawing at anything of his that was living, so that particles of him seemed to hover above his body like shiny metallic dust, finally reassembling to form a new and, if you enjoyed living, less improved Alex.

And then the getting used to it, the confusion of being stranded in between the living and the dead, waiting for the inevitable to happen, but not sure what that meant. He had heard stories of people in comas who wandered around like lost dogs until their bodies snatched their spirits back from the afterlife, only to live long productive lives. But then he remembered the hopeless look on the EMT's face and his matter-of-fact summation: "Well, at least he died fast." They didn't even try CPR. But still, still, perhaps currents of energy were sparking in the hidden gray recesses of his brain, little nooks and crannies scientists had yet to discover. What a disappointment for all those gathered on his lawn if, indeed, his body, wherever it was now, came back from the dead and showed up at school one day.

One thing he did know was that, at least for now, death really sucked. No bright lights or being led off to heaven by a bunch of bearded old guys in white robes.

Did that mean the other fate awaited, that devilish spirits were in meetings, making decisions about where Alex Youngblood should spend eternity?

Looking back at his past, he might've changed a few things, but not much. Granted, not many mourners were milling about, but what did they know? Alex had always believed that if there was a God, He'd be more mercenary than the one priests described. He liked the Old Testament kick-ass God better. That was a guy who would've understood the life he had constructed for himself until Maura freaked out. What did she expect to happen at Henry's party after she got drunk?

Still, he was surprised she hadn't come to check out his vigil, just as surprised as he'd been to see another dead kid, Ryan Holt, lurking in the shadows behind his house. Ryan had been killed in a car accident four months ago. Although dead longer, Ryan seemed closer to life than Alex, able to do more things, so maybe death could get better. Maybe Ryan was sent as a guide to help him through the transition, so that Alex might reclaim some semblance of his body—if only for a few weeks or months—before becoming permanently dead.

Alex was standing on his porch as Missy Rogers handed out candles. It made sense that she was the one who had organized this vigil. His whole life he had wanted to hook up with her, but she'd never go out with him. And yet there she was, passing out candles, always needing to do what she believed was the right thing. He should've been flattered, but he felt anger instead.

Tired of watching her, he decided to sit for a while. All he had on was a pair of tight blue jeans, and he wondered how he'd gotten into them. For two days he had walked around his house in the bloody clothes he'd been shot in. He watched his parents mourn in their own ways, though he'd never felt close to them. His sister came home from college but seemed annoyed that everything was taking so long. He heard her jabbering on the phone about some "hot guy" and a "fucking amazing" party she might have to miss.

And now no one was home but the live-in housekeeper.

His mother had lied to his aunt, saying she couldn't bear the pain of the vigil, and the whole family had gone to their vacation home on the Cape. Alex imagined them getting the house ready for the summer and taking the Sunfish out on the cove. If people knew, they'd say it was insensitive, but Alex would've done the same thing. The Youngbloods didn't believe in suffering. They were doers. You finished something, succeeded in it, and moved on. If everything fell apart, you just kept moving, extended the blinders, and made as much money as you could, so that anytime you felt like it, you could tell people to fuck off.

Alex looked at his arms and chest. Before the shooting, he'd already gotten tan from running with his shirt off, but now his skin was milky white, his veins branching out like thin, blue visible roots. He was still muscled, but to what end?

He was about to give in to the numbness sapping his spirit when the other kids showed up.

The dead ones.

* * *

"I know you," Frank Rizzo said to the man sitting nervously in his car.

The figure squirmed. It was James Keegan, who taught history to juniors and seniors at Frank's old high school.

"Calm down, Frank," the teacher said. "Kids are watching."

But Frank had no intention of calming down. "You should've stayed home, Mr. Keegan, instead of tracking Patti down like some horny pit bull."

"I'm here for the vigil," Mr. Keegan said, as if that proved his good intentions.

"Then why're you hiding in your car? Patti already told you to get lost." He looked around and located his sister. She was standing in the middle of Alex Youngblood's lawn, the wind catching her flimsy white dress and threatening to hoist her into the sky. She was spinning in circles, a beautiful pale whirling dervish. Was she just attracting attention to herself again, or was this some nutty ritual to bring Alex back from the dead?

123

Alex Youngblood! Why the fuss over that asshole?

"I just want to say something to her," Mr. Keegan said.

"I know you're a teacher," Frank said, "but if you get out of the car, I'm going to knock you out. I know what's been going on, so go home to your wife and baby."

Instead of responding, Mr. Keegan climbed out of the car and staggered like a sleepwalker in Patti's direction. He wore tan shorts, brown flip-flops, and a tight Under Armour T-shirt. He looked stronger than Frank had remembered, so Frank knew it wouldn't be easy to bring him down.

"I told you to stay in the car," Frank said.

But Mr. Keegan didn't seem to hear him.

Frank grabbed him by the arm. He understood why girls thought Mr. Keegan was hot, but now he looked like he hadn't slept in a week. His eyes were tired and bloodshot, and he seemed somewhat dazed.

"There's something wrong with her," Mr. Keegan said, pointing to Patti, as she spun pointlessly in circles.

"Yeah, she's crazy."

"You don't understand," Mr. Keegan said. "I want to help her."

"Then get back in the car."

By now, kids were looking at them.

"I just need to talk to her," Mr. Keegan said.

"Then call her later. This stupid vigil's almost over anyway."

But Mr. Keegan kept walking, so Frank had no choice but to tackle him.

* * *

It was Campbell McVeigh's idea to go to the vigil. His father had told him he could take three six-packs as long as he and his friends were "discreet" and drank them in the woods beforehand. After all, his father and his friends had done things like that, so what was the harm, and his father knew the Youngbloods well, especially Alex. Alex would've liked his friends to mourn his death with an impromptu party. Maybe even get tattoos to commemorate the years the boys had played sports together.

So between the beer and the pot that his friend George Humphreys had brought, Campbell and his friends were feeling pretty good when Missy Rogers started to hand out candles. Everything would've gone smoothly if this geek, Robert Hammersmith, a short kid with black curly hair, hadn't tried to hit on Missy, and if Hammersmith's even geekier friend, a tall kid named Barney Roth, hadn't shot off his mouth. Campbell had watched Hammersmith all night. Like he was worthy of Missy, Campbell thought. I mean, come on.

"Do you believe that little prick," Campbell said, taking a toke from a joint.

"He's okay," Tyler Whitney said.

Tyler was one of them but always tried to be fair to everyone, which was why he was class president or vice president every year. In spite of that, Campbell put up with him because they'd been teammates since first grade.

"You aren't going to start that nice-guy shit again, are you?" Campbell said.

"I'm just saying that these other kids probably don't get why we're partying."

"Who cares?"

"I do," Tyler said.

A few other guys agreed with Tyler and asked Campbell to tone it down.

But when George Humphreys likened Missy's vigil candles to rectal thermometers, and Campbell said they resembled dildos, Hammersmith's friend, the kid named Barney, was dumb enough to compare Campbell and his friends to monkeys playing with their shit. That's when Hammersmith asked if he could help Missy, and that really pissed off Campbell because he knew that if Alex were alive he would've thrown these assholes off his property.

After that, there was some arguing until Hammersmith and Missy and the kid named Barney walked away. But Campbell was still mad. He went quiet, like he always did before a fight. He eyed his backpack, thinking about his father's Glock, which was hidden under some gym clothes. He'd been carrying it around for months, not exactly sure why,

125

though knowing this wasn't the right time to use it. Still, he had to unload on someone, right?—preferably Roth. That's what he was about to do when he felt a hand on his shoulder.

"Chill, dude."

It was Tyler.

"Just can't stop thinking about how that tall guy dissed me," Campbell said.

"You're drunk, Campbell. A little touchy."

Campbell looked around until he spotted the kid named Barney, who had moved about twenty yards away. "I need to talk to that guy. Any of you have my back?"

"I do," George Humphreys said, though all the rest stayed quiet.

"Well, I'm outta here," Tyler said. "But I'm telling you, Alex wouldn't have wanted this."

"We talking about the same Alex?"

"Whatever. I'm gone," Tyler said, then headed toward the street.

After Tyler left, Campbell complained for about ten minutes before letting it drop. Most of the beer had been drunk, and there was only one joint left, which got passed around. When everyone started to leave, Campbell and his friends got up and stretched, as if warming up before a big game. They probably would've gone home peacefully if Campbell hadn't noticed two guys arguing in front of a car parked illegally on the street.

"What's *that* about?" he said, moving toward the commotion.

* * *

Jim Keegan stared at himself in the bedroom mirror, wondering who this twenty-six-year-old stranger was. He was getting ready to drive to an outdoor vigil for Alex Youngblood, a student of his who had been inexplicably murdered two nights ago. It seemed like a nice gesture—a teacher comforting his students—but Jim knew he was going for another reason. He had overheard Patti Rizzo say she'd be there, and he needed to see her.

"What time will you be home?" his wife asked. She was holding the baby. She looked tired but, as always, beautiful. She was intelligent, too, and nice, and thoughtful, and unselfish. Yet here he was, going off in the middle of the night, hoping to catch a glimpse of one of his female students.

"I won't be long," he said. "Promise." He went over and kissed her on the forehead, then bent down to kiss the baby, who looked up with vacant blue eyes.

"It's so sad what happened to that boy," his wife said. "I hope a student didn't do it."

"It's too early to know," he said.

In fact, he didn't care much for Alex Youngblood. He'd always been disruptive in class, making dumb jokes and flirting with girls, especially Patti. In a way (and this thought made him feel ashamed), the last few weeks of school would be easier with Alex gone. He wouldn't have to endure pangs of jealousy while watching Alex try his sophomoric moves on Patti.

It had been hard enough dealing with the mind-numbing exhaustion he'd felt since the baby was born. Both he and his wife were working, so they took turns holding and rocking the child in the middle of the night, which wasn't easy because of the casts that, like the outer shells of a crab, imprisoned his tiny legs. He'd been born early with his feet turned inward. There was the possibility of club foot, the doctors had said, so only hours after his birth, the doctors had molded his feet into the proper position, then set them with casts that had to be cut off and replaced every week to compensate for his growth. On top of that, the baby was colicky, so he cried and constantly spit up.

Still, Jim loved his wife and son. He even loved his job—that rush of walking into a noisy classroom and taking it over by making a joke, or blowing students away with some outrageous historical fact. He didn't want them to think history was dry and boring.

At first, he was taken by Patti's beauty, intrigued by her dreaminess, by the way she'd stare off into nothingness, sucking in her cheeks as if she were sipping from a straw. But he was used to performing in front of beautiful blond and blue-eyed girls. His school district seemed to breed them like exotic butterflies. She was in no way one of his best students. She rarely spoke, and when she did, her answers were vague, as if he'd caught her in the middle of a daydream.

But everything changed when he introduced the class to Heloise and Abelard. It started while the class was reviewing the importance of the Catholic Church during the Middle Ages, and a student, Barney Roth, a likable wise guy, said, "Time to snooze." Then another student, Lucille Gorski, ranted about how the Church had always persecuted women but none of them had the power to fight back.

It was then that he decided to give a few lessons on Heloise and Abelard. He retold their story, how the monk-priest Abelard seduced his student Heloise, how they became obsessed with each other, the story ending tragically with Abelard, a broken man and full of guilt, being castrated by a posse of men sent by Heloise's uncle.

"Ouch," Barney Roth had said, as Jim explained the symbolism of the act.

Jim was proud of how he had prepared for the next two classes by finding letters between the lovers. And his strategy worked. By peopling the historical period with flesh-and-blood characters, he was able to talk about Church history, philosophy, and the sexual conduct of the time. At the end of his lectures he gave a two-sentence creative writing assignment: "Let's say that the last letter between Abelard and Heloise has never been found. Choose one of these characters and write that undiscovered letter."

As expected, all of the boys wrote from Abelard's point of view, painfully detailing Abelard's sexual frustration. Sometimes these letters were crude, using phrases that were probably stolen from porn sites; other times, inventive, one boy describing the flagellations Abelard would daily inflict on himself to forget his memories of Heloise's flesh. The girls tried a bit harder, but except for Lucille Gorski's threat to have Abelard beheaded, most of the letters sounded like a medley of mushy twitters from a *Seventeen* magazine site.

And then he read Patti Rizzo's letter.

She began with "Music is God, and God is Music. And you are my Music and my God." She continued in one long unbroken sentence, sometimes chastising Abelard, other times teasing him with sexual language and imagery. Jim became aroused as he read her letter and made comments on it, praising her for this image or that turn of phrase. It wasn't until later that he realized he was writing Abelard's part of the correspondence. That became clear after Patti began to leave more letters on his desk. They were, she said, part of her final project. Instead of writing a traditional paper, she had asked to compose Heloise's secret journal. How could he refuse such an imaginative proposal? And everything would've been fine if he had kept himself from scribbling inappropriate comments in the margins.

It was a silly and stupid thing to do. He was supposed to be the teacher, the mature one. So he was surprised as anyone to find himself almost groaning whenever he saw Patti drifting ghostlike down the hallways, as if in a trance, pressing her composition notebook to her small breasts. He had no idea if she knew what she was doing, until she asked to stay for extra help. The next time they met, it was at a coffee shop, and then a few nights later at a secluded spot near Echo Pond, where they made love.

And that's when it all ended as abruptly as it had started. She wouldn't see him outside of class, and when he tried to stop her in the hall, she'd just smile and fake confusion, as if it were the first time she'd ever laid eyes on him.

He felt humiliated and angry, yet here he was at Alex Youngblood's vigil, willing to risk everything to touch her hair or to inhale the perfume he had bought her.

* * *

Strange things were happening as Alex sat on the porch: kids arguing with each other, more commotion near a car parked in front of his house, candles being lit, which for some reason hurt his eyes. But none of this seemed important when the dead ones arrived, so beautiful and pale. So seemingly harmless.

There was one dead girl who seemed in charge. She glided up to him, swaying elegantly like a seahorse. This one he was afraid of. Her hair was black and damp, as if she had just stepped out of the shower. She looked confident, her eyes the flat black of charcoal, taking him in. But then she spotted Ryan Holt and floated toward him.

That's when the other two girls appeared. They were more to Alex's liking, pale like the first one, but blond with huge blue eyes and eternal smiles. They whispered unintelligibly in a pleasant rhythmic language, then tried to lift him a few inches off the ground. He hovered there, surprised to discover he could make himself rise or fall just by thinking on it. He saw the black-haired girl again, who was now leading Ryan into the woods. Just before they disappeared, she turned and gave Alex an evil glare.

Poor Ryan, he thought. What must he have done to deserve that girl?

Then he found himself floating above everyone, with the girls at his side.

They gestured for him to follow.

And he did.

* * *

Frank was surprised Mr. Keegan didn't struggle when he tackled him. He straddled his waist and hit him a few times in the face. He probably would've continued to pound away if Campbell McVeigh and his friends hadn't shown up.

"What're you doing, dude?" Campbell said. "He's a teacher."

When Frank looked up, Mr. Keegan took advantage of the distraction to break free. Frank's eyes moved from him to Campbell and then to Patti. She had stopped twirling and was taking in the scene, probably enjoying it. "What a bitch!" Frank said.

"That's your sister, dude," Campbell said. "Lighten up."

Frank was so hyped up he could hardly breathe. "Fuck off, McVeigh."

"Whoa," George Humphreys, one of Campbell's friends, said. "Can't really talk to us like that, dude."

Frank turned to locate Mr. Keegan again and was angry to discover that he was halfway to Patti. He ran after the teacher until Campbell and his friends blocked his way.

"You don't even know what the fuck's going on," Frank said.

"Not hard to figure out," Campbell said.

"Just get out of the way."

Campbell shook his head. "I don't think so."

130

"Why?"

"Why not?"

"Don't be a prick, Campbell," Frank said, deciding to make a bolt between Campbell and George Humphreys. He took two steps before George hit him in the face, and then the other guys jumped in.

* * *

So Mr. Keegan's been screwing Patti Rizzo, Campbell thought. Campbell probably wouldn't have cared, but then Frank had to shoot off his mouth, so they were forced to teach him a lesson, until Mr. Keegan broke it up. Campbell had never liked the teacher, which was partly why he slid the middle finger of his right hand in and out of a circle he made with the thumb and forefinger of his left hand. "Shame on you, Mr. Keegan," he said. "Who woulda thought?"

Half an hour later, Campbell found himself sitting on the fifty-yard line of the football field, drinking a beer he had put aside. "What a night!" he said.

"Yeah," George said. "This one's going to take time to process."

"It would've been perfect if we could've given Hammersmith a beatdown," Campbell said. "Still can't believe he was sniffing around Missy."

George agreed.

Then Campbell pointed toward a figure jogging around the track. "Who's that?"

"It's Tyler," George said.

Campbell stumbled toward the jogger, and when Tyler saw them he stopped, trying to catch his breath.

"What are ya doin'?" Campbell asked.

"Trying to run off tonight's stink."

"You missed a good fight."

Tyler was sweating and still breathing hard. "You didn't beat up Hammersmith, did you?"

"Why? You guys gay lovers?"

Tyler shook his head. "Look, I just wanna finish my run, so leave me the fuck alone."

"What's your problem?"

"Just tired. Of you, high school. Everything. Can't wait until September, when I can get out of here."

"Because of tonight?"

"Can't say. But tomorrow I'm going to apologize to Hammersmith for the stuff you spouted at him."

"Why don't you give him a blow job while you're at it?" Campbell said.

And that's when the lights went out for Campbell. He lay half-conscious on his back, gazing into the clear night. He thought he saw a few white shapes pass overhead, but he guessed that's what people meant when they talked about "seeing stars."

* * *

As Jim Keegan staggered toward Patti Rizzo she began to twirl again, either to excite him or to keep him away.

After tonight, he knew, his life would never be the same. Too many kids were there, too many wondering why their history teacher, bleeding from the mouth, was standing next to Patti. Too many witnessing his fight with Frank. He could say he came out of concern for Alex and then became worried by Patti's strange behavior and dance. It would be a stretch, but he might still pull it off if he left right then.

"I can take you home," he found himself saying.

She kept spinning, and as he reached out to her she collapsed onto the ground. He knelt next to her, but she pushed him away, laughing. Then he saw a commotion near his car. It was Campbell McVeigh and his friends beating up Frank Rizzo, and although he knew Frank probably deserved it, he ran to break it up. After everyone had calmed down, he tried to compose himself and find Patti, but she was gone. He was tired and anxious and scared, so he got into his car and sped away. No more than a block from Alex's house, he gripped the steering wheel and started to cry. He would have to tell his wife everything now. And then what? There were so many grim possibilities that the smart thing would've been to get on I-95 North and not look back.

Instead, he drove aimlessly around, his ancient red Toyota laboring up and down steep hills, groaning like an old refrigerator. He eventually ended up in a parking lot behind the local convenience store. He shut off the engine and sat there. No one seemed to be around, except for a dark figure to his right, who was sitting on a small garbage can under a dim light, smoking a cigarette. Jim lowered his backrest, then closed his eyes, replaying the events of the night. At the part where Frank Rizzo tackled him, he was jolted from his reverie by a knock on the driver's side window. He opened his eyes to see a boy's smiling face about a foot from his own.

Jim rolled down the window, and the boy said, "I thought that was you, Mr. Keegan. I got worried because you weren't moving. I thought you might've stroked out or something."

Jim stared long and hard at the boy, finally recognizing him as Richard Peterson, a black kid students called X-Ray. "No, I'm okay, Richard."

"You sure? You look like you've been crying."

"It's been a long night."

Richard took a drag from his cigarette, then turned and blew the smoke behind him. "Yeah, I've sure had my share of those."

"You mind if I borrow a smoke?" Jim asked.

Richard looked startled but said, "Sure."

Jim got out of the car and followed the boy to the area by the garbage can, where they both sat down, their backs against a brick wall.

"I'm surprised you smoke," Richard said.

"I usually don't."

"I got back into it a few months ago. It's supposed to hype you up, but it kind of relaxes me."

Jim borrowed Richard's cigarette to light his own. He inhaled deeply, surprised at how good it tasted. "You want me to call you Richard or X-Ray?"

"For some reason Richard works better with you."

Jim watched the boy take a drag. He had always thought Richard was a curious kid. He had missed his share of classes, but when he came, he did the work. Jim was told early in September that Richard had an anxiety disorder, which was being managed with medication.

133

Sometimes, though, the wheels came off the track, like the time Richard wrote a paper for Jim's class arguing that Tupac Shakur's murder was a conspiracy engineered by evangelicals.

"Are you going to graduation?" Jim asked.

"I dunno. I don't think I'd be missed."

"I'm beginning to think the same about me."

"No, Mr. Keegan, you're the best. There's not much I'll remember about high school except all the cool shit you did in class."

"Will you do me a favor, Richard?" Jim asked.

"Sure."

"Remember that cool shit because you might feel differently about me in a few days."

Richard looked confused.

"I've done a few things I wish I hadn't," Jim said.

"Oh yeah, I sure get that."

"Get what?"

"I dunno. Sometimes I think we're all waiting at this huge bus station, and some people get on the bus that's going to Las Vegas, while others are on the one that breaks down in the middle of someplace stupid like Kansas. And then there's me, who ends up on the bus that disappears into a tunnel and never comes out."

Jim laughed. "Well, save me a seat, Richard, and maybe we'll survive the crash together."

"See, Mr. Keegan, you always come out with something cool."

"Not really. The bus metaphor was yours."

Richard stood. He seemed pleased with himself. "You're the last person I would've thought had problems," he said. "It almost makes me feel good about myself. If you want I can give you a Xanax. It's a low dose, so it makes you chill, not comatose." He removed a pill from the watch pocket of his jeans.

Jim hesitated, then took the white oval tablet and wedged it under his tongue. He pointed to a Dunkin' Donuts across the street. "Why don't we get a coffee and split some Munchkins."

"That'd be cool, though the caffeine will fuck with the Xanax," Richard said, then caught himself. "Sorry, Mr. Keegan. I meant no disrespect."

"No problem, Richard, but let's do it anyway. Then I have to get home."

"Yeah, how's your baby? You always used to talk about him. Man, did you look tired after he was born. I'm an insomniac, so I know how that messes with your head."

"Yeah, but you get used to it."

"You can get used to most anything if you try hard enough, Mr. Keegan. You can even get used to stuff you don't want to get used to."

Jim didn't agree with Richard about that, but he didn't feel like leading anyone out of the darkness tonight. All he knew was that he was hungry and needed to be home, where he could go to the baby's room and rock him until they both fell asleep.

* * *

For the first time, Alex didn't mind being dead. It was actually kind of fun, drifting above the town with two beautiful girls, sometimes caught in the draft of their seductive maneuvers as they plunged into the silent music of the night. Other times, he went off on his own but only so far, for fear of crossing paths with the black-haired girl, the one with the charcoal eyes.

He could smell the night air, almost taste the dew dampening the grass below. And oh, how he wanted these two girls.

He sailed over Echo Pond, not saddened when he recognized the spot where he'd been shot. He traveled over the bordering woods, noticing a lone figure walking through a path, banging on trees with what looked like a baseball bat. It was Adam Igoe, a poor, tough kid from his football team. From there he headed for the football field, wanting to see it one last time. He was surprised to find Campbell and Tyler and the other guys there, even more surprised when Tyler knocked out Campbell with one punch. In a way, he wanted to know why, but who cared anymore? There was this night, and the flying, and the two girls suddenly appearing next to him. This time they were naked and teasing him, and when they took flight, he followed, ending up in a cemetery he'd never seen before. The girls stood to the left of a

135

tombstone with Phineas McGee etched on it. To the right was an old man in a white waistcoat that covered a ruffled white shirt. He wore white breeches, knee-high socks, and black leather shoes fastened with buckles. A wide-brimmed hat turned up on three sides covered his pale wig. He looked very tired.

"Who are you?" Alex said.

"I could ask the same question," the old man said.

Alex thought this was some kind of initiation, that the girls wanted him to see the terrible afterlives of some of the dead before leading him away to have fun. So he decided to play along.

"Where are the others?"

The old man gestured toward the ground. "They'll be along soon."

"How old are you?"

The old man looked confused, then pointed to the dates on his tombstone, which suggested he lived three hundred years ago.

"Can't you leave?" Alex asked.

"No one leaves here."

Alex laughed. "So what did you do to be trapped for eternity?"

"Don't remember," the old man said. Then he sat down on a large rock next to his grave, and that's when the others began to appear, dressed in clothes from many different ages. They were an unhappy lot, curiously taking Alex in. They looked like they wanted to hurt him but couldn't figure out how. He turned his attention to the girls again, who floated near a tall obelisk. "I'm ready," he said.

"We know," they whispered.

"No, I mean I'm ready, you know, for anything."

"Yes, yes," they hissed, still smiling, waving their fingers at him as if to say, "Naughty, naughty boy."

And then they vanished.

He tried to follow them, tried to lift off and escape into the sky, but he couldn't.

And in one terrifying, frozen moment, the dead were upon him.

THE DHARMA WHEEL

One Saturday late in May, while waiting for the bus on Route 114, Rishi Patil heard the tire of a passing tractor-trailer explode. To him, that's what the shot that had killed Alex Youngblood sounded like. He didn't have to ask who fired it because he saw Maura McManus, faintly silhouetted by a lamp near a water fountain, pull the gun from her hoodie. He saw Alex move toward her, laugh, then stroll away. Which is when Maura appeared to trip and lurch forward, setting off a flash that lit up the night. The gun fell from her hand to the ground, and she quickly retrieved it and ran off.

Rishi knew he should've come forward that night, and if not then, certainly by now, but some moral impulse he couldn't explain had kept him silent. Was it the surprise Maura showed when the gun went off? Was it because he had never liked Alex, who had a sleazebag reputation with girls and who'd always made fun of Rishi and his friends?

One side of him wanted to know more facts; another side wished he had taken a different route home that night; and still another felt a profound sadness that a human being had been killed. He knew he couldn't keep silent much longer—guilt worming its way into his every waking moment.

Now, more than a week later, about an hour from dusk, after spotting Maura buying a bag of sunflower seeds at the convenience store, he followed her to the exact place where Alex had been shot. She sat on a boulder near the water's edge, staring, as if into nothingness. As he watched her, he thought about the conversation he'd had earlier in the evening with Barney Roth and Lucille Gorski. They were in Barney's basement, lounging on beanbag chairs next to a pool table.

"'Existing is plagiarism,'" Barney had said, smiling as he quoted from a book he cradled in both hands.

"What's that supposed to mean?" Lucille said.

"Well, listen to these gems. 'Nothing makes us modest, not even the sight of a corpse.' Or this one: 'To *be* is to be cornered.'"

Rishi laughed. "That certainly clears up a lot."

"I thought that with all the Hindu shit you read you'd like this guy," Barney said, holding up the book. "You gotta be patient with these aphorisms, let them wash over you."

If anyone else had referred to Rishi's beliefs as "Hindu shit," Rishi would've punched them out. But Barney was just as likely to call the movement of the planets and stars "astronomy shit," or the symbolism of Shakespeare's plays "Shakespeare shit." Rishi had once even heard him criticize a kid in the cafeteria for buying into "that Caesar salad shit" philosophy of eating instead of wolfing down a few slices of pizza.

In contrast to Rishi, Lucille wasn't so accepting of Barney's new obsession: depressing philosophical aphorisms from a guy named E. M. Cioran.

"They sound like something you'd hear in those old hippie movies that run at two in the morning," Lucille said. "You know, when everyone drops acid and says dumb things. Let me look at that book," she said, wresting it away from Barney. "*The Trouble with Being Born.* Now there's an uplifting title." Barney tried to reclaim the book but Lucille held on tight. "And now let's read about Mr. Cioran. It says he's a 'poet-philosopher whose uncompromising pessimism is finally becoming the world's generalized state of mind. Yet his work is refreshing and invigorating.' I get the first part, but I don't see what's refreshing about anything you just read."

"That's because you're naïve enough to think your life matters," Barney said.

"Is this the dude who killed himself?" Rishi asked.

"Actually, he lived into his eighties."

"And the whole book's full of these pessimistic—"

"Realistic."

"—tidbits?"

Barney snatched the book back from Lucille. "Just one more," he said, flipping the pages until he found what he was looking for. "'A book should open old wounds, even inflict new ones. A book should be a *danger*.' I think what he's saying is, 'Don't be afraid to spend a couple of days with this book. It's not wrong to think the world sucks, and it doesn't mean you should kill yourself. Maybe you'll live a better life if you decide to go on in spite of the fact that everything's pointless.'"

"Yeah, yeah, yeah," Lucile said. "The same old crap. Is there a God? Why do we get up in the morning? Why be good when being bad is so much fun? You know, Barney, you were fun until your brother started sending you books from college. But at least you've convinced me not to waste my time on Introduction to Philosophy next year."

"This coming from the girlfriend of a guy who thinks he can film ghosts. Now that's a real waste of time."

"Well, at least Marty's an upbeat guy."

"Yeah, obsessing about dead people will do that to you."

This back-and-forth was giving Rishi a headache but he decided to get his two cents in. "I think what Lucille means, Barney, is that these aphorisms are just word games, what you used to call 'mind fucks,' until you became enlightened. I liked it better when you were harping about aliens creating us."

"I didn't say aliens created us. I'm smarter than that. What I said is that we could easily be no more than playthings in someone's or some thing's personal video game. A consciousness that we'll never be able to fathom because to them we're a species lower than navel lint. Maybe we're not even a species but a bunch of pixels banging off each other like billiard balls." He pointed to the balls scattered on the pool table, then leaned over and rolled the cue ball into three striped balls resting harmlessly near a side pocket.

"If that's true," Lucille said, "how can someone as insignificant as you figure it out? I mean, you're just a bunch of pixels?"

"Maybe they've given limited insights to some of their creations, using them to enlighten or distract the others. Yeah, maybe all our thoughts and actions are part of an experiment we have no control over. I mean, wouldn't that piss you off?"

"No offense, Barney," Rishi said, "but I think you're making this stuff up as you go along. And even if you're right, what does it matter?"

"That's where Cioran comes in. If you have to wake up every morning and stare into the abyss, you might as well poke fun at it."

Lucille started to laugh, but Rishi didn't find much of Barney's speculating funny. Many times he had wondered about the meaning of life. Barney misunderstood what he called Rishi's "Hindu shit." Even Rishi didn't grasp everything that had been thrown at him, piecemeal, over the years, but he did believe in karma, in the importance of making the right moral decisions. "We are the heirs of our own actions," Buddha had said, which made a hell of a lot more sense than Cioran's gloomy aphorisms.

"Are you listening to me, Reesh?" Barney said.

"I always listen to you, Barney."

"I've never understood why," Lucille said. "Sorry, guys, but I have to meet Marty."

"Dining with ghosts tonight?" Barney said.

"They're not really ghosts, Barney. They're figments of Marty's imagination that don't exist because, according to you, Marty's nothing but a bunch of pixels created by Bill Fucking Gates."

"Very good, Lucille, but Gates is a bunch of pixels, too."

"Oh, fuck you."

"Fuck you back," Barney said playfully.

"Can you guys stop with the swearing?" Rishi said. "Don't know why you always go on like that." Rishi was raised in a house where people rarely yelled and never swore, so when others did, he felt uncomfortable. In his house, words were very powerful and you weren't supposed to abuse the privilege of using them.

"Sorry, Reesh," Lucille said. She went over and kissed him on the cheek, then shot Barney the finger on her way upstairs.

"I like that girl," Barney said. "Wish I'd asked her out before Marty did."

Rishi laughed at the thought of Barney and Lucille kayaking

peacefully on Echo Pond.

"What's so funny?"

"For a guy who thinks he knows everything, you're incredibly clueless."

"Like I said, maybe I have no control over that."

"If you ever rob a bank," Rishi said, "I wouldn't use 'I'm just a jumble of pixels' as a defense."

"You weren't fucking listening, Reesh."

"I'm always fucking listening to you, Barney. That's why we're friends."

Barney smiled. "I can see why you don't like swearing, Reesh. You're not very good at it. It's like listening to a nun try to rap. But let's get back to the alien stuff...."

Rather than listen to another stupid theory, Rishi distracted Barney by racking the billiard balls and grabbing a cue. They played for about half an hour; then Rishi left. Hungry, he stopped at Rite Aid for a Clif Bar, and that's when he saw Maura McManus and followed her to the scene of the murder.

She had her back to him, tossing pebbles into the water, fixated on something only she could see, while a few cormorants periodically surfaced after diving deep for trout.

Rishi stopped about ten feet from her. "Fishermen really hate those birds," he said.

Maura stood and turned, seemingly confused until she recognized him. "Rishi, right?"

"Yeah, we both did cross-country and used to have a few classes together."

"And then you wound up in AP."

"Yeah."

"Why did you quit cross-country?"

"Got into baseball, so I started playing Fall Ball and couldn't do both." Here he was, a few feet away from where Maura had shot Alex Youngblood, and they were talking about high school sports.

"What were you saying about those birds?" Maura asked.

"They're cormorants. They usually don't come in this far, but now

141

they're eating all the trout, which is making fishermen mad."

"Do you fish?'

"A little."

"That must be fun," she said, though there was no emotion in her words.

In the past, Rishi had noticed Maura a number of times. He was sure that when people saw him they always associated him with Barney and Lucille and a few other kids, but he couldn't remember Maura hanging out with any particular group. Which surprised him. It wasn't as if she were homely or one of those kids who, being so timid, looked like they might shatter into pieces when you talked to them. In fact, Rishi had always thought she was pretty. He believed real beauty came from imperfection, which was why all the perfectly beautiful girls at school, the ones who could be models or invited to an invitation-only Taylor Swift luncheon, the ones who walked with short, choppy steps as if they had soccer balls wedged between their knees, didn't do much for him. Like many of those girls, Maura had silky brown hair, high cheekbones, and almond-colored big brown eyes, but the Creator had forgotten (thankfully, from Rishi's point of view) to give her one of those tiny noses that seem to turn up so very, very slightly at its tip. In contrast, Maura had a prominent Roman nose, making her look almost Mediterranean and sophisticated, though she didn't seem too sophisticated now. Instead, she looked worn out and a little spacey. She kept staring at him, and he felt if he didn't speak they might stand there for hours, examining each other.

"Are you okay?" he asked.

She came back from wherever she had vanished to. "Yeah, just a little tired."

"I feel the same. I think I'll sleep for about a week after graduation, a kind of collapse after four years of grinding away."

Maura looked surprised. "I always thought school was easy for kids like you."

"No, I work hard at it."

"Hmm."

Rishi felt like he was losing her again, so he decided to get to the point. "I saw you faint in the hall last week. I'm sorry about Alex."

She moved back a step. "I hardly knew him."

"Weren't you two going out?"

"Is that what people think?"

"Sorry, I thought that's why you were here," Rishi said.

"You knew he was shot here?"

"Everyone does."

"Who do you think did it?" Maura said.

Rishi thought long and hard before answering her question. "Some kids say punks from Riverside did it," he said. "Everyone knows that Alex could tick people off."

"But he could be nice, too."

Considering all the lousy things he saw Alex do over four years of high school, he wondered if they were talking about the same Alex. "I guess you'd know," was all he could say.

"Maybe someone passing through did it," she offered. "You know, like a serial killer."

"I think it was an accident," Rishi said.

Maura suddenly seemed interested, so he continued.

"When was the last time anyone was killed in this town? I think they'll find out one of his friends was playing with a gun, or something stupid like that. I mean, go on the Internet. Kids are getting killed all the time in fluke accidents. Eventually someone will confess, or the cops will find the gun."

"There are a lot of places to hide a gun," Maura said.

"Someone will come forward."

"Why are you so sure?"

"How do you live with something like that?"

Maura went silent again. She moved back to the boulder and leaned against it, and Rishi joined her. There wasn't much room, so their thighs almost touched and he could smell her perfume. She reached into a front pocket of her jeans and pulled out a bag of sunflower seeds, offering him some. "Thanks," he said, taking a handful. Then he asked if the police had questioned her.

"Yeah," she said, "but I told them Alex and I broke up a few weeks ago."

"Was that true?"

"Of course it's true." She looked out onto the water again. "If it ends up being an accident," she said, "what do you think they'll do to the shooter? I mean, the police would have to take that person's word because Alex is dead."

"Not if there was an eyewitness."

"But what if there wasn't?"

"There's always a witness."

"How do you know so much about this stuff?"

Rishi wanted to say, "Because I was there that night," but he couldn't get the words out.

"I'm just throwing out theories," he said. "A lot matters, too, if it was self-defense. Maybe Alex attacked the shooter that night, or had done something like that in the past. Maybe the shooter was afraid of him."

"What does it matter now?" Maura said. "He's dead."

"Like I said, it depends on what you can live with."

Maura lost control of the bag of seeds and it fell to the ground. She seemed agitated, so Rishi reached over and touched her arm. "I can go if you want."

Maura knelt and picked up the bag. "No, I don't want to be alone right now." She leaned back on the boulder, and Rishi was surprised when she rested her head on his shoulder, even more surprised when he saw some tears on her cheeks. He put his arm around her, and she started to cry, though not hard enough to attract attention.

"You probably think I'm nuts," she said.

"No, I think you're sad."

"You'll never know just *how* sad." She reached over and grabbed his hand, holding on to it very tightly. "You don't have to stay long. Just give me a few minutes to get it together."

"I'll stay as long as you want."

"Why?"

"It's the way I am."

As he sat there, his eyes followed a cormorant, who kept taking dive after dive, refusing to quit until it surfaced with a trout. Then an early-evening kayaker passed and waved at them. Rishi knew he'd eventually have to tell Maura what he saw that night. She stumbled, he would say, and the gun went off, an accident, plain and simple. But he also sensed there was more to the story, that she had been terribly wronged by Alex. With his arm around her, he could almost feel this unknown injury working out its ugliness inside her.

"Can I buy you a Froyo or something?" he asked.

She stood again, trying to compose herself. "I probably should get home, Rishi."

"My friends call me Reesh."

She smiled. "Am I your friend?"

"I'll let you know after you split a Froyo with me." He held out his hand, and she took it.

"I promise not to cry there," she said.

"That'd probably be a good idea."

* * *

It was around four in the afternoon and raining hard outside, the wind so fierce against Maura's bedroom window that water leaked through a few panes that needed to be caulked. She was sitting on her bed. She had the remaining five bullets spread out on the comforter, just as she had the day she'd bought the gun. The gun rested quietly next to the bullets. She thought she had wiped it clean of dirt and mud, but there was still soil caked around the trigger. She took a tissue from her bed stand and rubbed the curved piece of metal, watching specks of dirt float into the air before settling onto the comforter.

She was deciding what to do with the gun.

Two days ago, on the bike path, Rishi Patil had made her realize that someone might find it, so she dug it up. It was as if Rishi had been sent that day to guide her, yet, inexplicably, she'd been avoiding him, saying she needed time to think. She didn't know what to make of Rishi, and she didn't understand why she'd left the bike path with him to get a frozen yogurt. The whole thing was ludicrous. Would he even speak to her if he knew what she had done, though even he had thought it was an accident? And maybe it was. Maybe she'd forgotten about the one bullet she had left in the chamber. She had just wanted to scare Alex. All she remembered was Alex taunting her, which brought back the laughter of the boys at his cousin Henry's house as they talked and snapped pictures. That's why she kept pulling the trigger until, instead of a click, she heard a thunderous echo that made her whole body convulse, as if she'd been leaning against a cannon as it went off.

On the bike path, and later at the yogurt shop, Rishi kept steering the conversation back to the shooting. At first that scared her, but then she became the one who started to ask questions. She couldn't understand why he was so certain the shooter would confess.

"I guess I was raised a certain way," Rishi had said.

"But what would the shooter have to gain?"

"Happiness?"

"In jail?"

"Only if he had killed Alex in cold blood."

She remembered Rishi sitting across from her. He had soft, dark, unblemished skin and sleepy eyes. She had questioned him about his idea of happiness, which made him borrow a pencil from the counter person at Froyo and draw a crude picture of what he called the Dharma Wheel on the back of a paper menu.

"Don't laugh," he said as he sketched.

"Why would I do that?"

What he ended up sliding over to Maura was a drawing of a wheel with eight spokes branching out from a large hub. "I can't explain everything I've read about this wheel," he said, "but I think the general idea is that each spoke represents a path to what some people call enlightenment. You know, some kind of self-understanding, and that's important because we're all connected in some way. We have to try to make the right choices even if the results suck." He seemed frustrated as he struggled to find the right words.

"Did your parents teach you that?" Maura asked.

"No, they're not very religious. My grandfather told me about the Dharma Wheel, so I've been reading up on it and on other things. Just think about it for a few days, okay?"

So she tried, but she could only get so far before fear and guilt returned to take turns punishing her. All she really wanted was to see Rishi again, and it seemed unfair that she hadn't met him a year ago. Everything was so messed up, as if a few spokes of Rishi's wheel were broken or missing. When he walked her back to the bike path that night, he said it was important for her to call him, that he had something to tell her and that it couldn't wait much longer.

She got off the bed and walked over to her bedroom window, wondering what that "something" was. It was still raining hard, a foot-wide river of water threatening to spill over the concrete curb. It was supposed to let up by dinnertime, and she hoped Rishi would be free by then. She went back and sat on her bed. She grabbed her cell phone and looked up his number but couldn't bring herself to call. Then the bullets reclaimed her attention, their tips like points of a pinwheel. She waited, as if expecting them to start whirling, perhaps spin so fast that she'd be caught up in their frenzy and carried away.

But they lay, motionless—five small arrows pointing in different directions.

She knew she had to choose one.

EPILOGUE

Campbell McVeigh had been on his way home from Barney Roth's house when he heard the shot that (as he would discover later) had killed his best friend, Alex Youngblood. Just minutes before, he'd been hiding in the bushes, pointing his father's Glock at Barney Roth's skinny-ass frame as Barney dragged some garbage cans down his driveway toward the sidewalk. Campbell was no doubt the only kid in his senior class who had pulled the trigger on a handgun on a weekly basis, usually when the noise between his ears got so loud that he needed a louder noise to keep him from doing something crazy. But now, the temporary fix he got from the boom and recoil of shooting at the range was wearing off. The whisperings and murmurs kept getting louder. Boom! Boom! Boom! Why hadn't he just offed Roth, then taken himself out? No suicide note. No nothin'. Just a lot of questions for dumbass kids to think about for a year or two. Whatever, he wasn't going to make the same mistake twice.

* * *

Barney Roth was feeling pretty good about himself, so good he decided to meet some friends at a Sunday night concert at the town beach. Normally, he hated doing anything everyone else did, even if it was something he found interesting, but the group that was playing was fairly cool, a trio that wasn't quite rap, and wasn't quite rock or grunge, so they somehow appealed to everyone, even though the lead singer had said publicly that he "didn't give a fuck" about his audience. Barney had to admire that kind of arrogance. That's the way he felt about his drawing. Art for art's sake, and the hell *with everyone else. He was halfway to the beach when he decided to grab a water at Cumberland Farms, so he swerved his father's old Altima into the parking lot.*

* * *

Campbell had decided to walk to the concert. He had the Glock wedged between his back and the waistband of his red seersucker shorts, the weapon made invisible by the baggy black Vineyard Vines T-shirt he'd thrown on. He was happy, no, actually relieved, to be stumbling toward the abyss, every nerve in his brain on fire. No pot, or Percs, or Xanax, could dull the rage now. Muscle memory had gotten him through football and baseball for part of the year, and getting nasty with girls had helped with the rest. But when Alex got shot, everything came apart. Alex was the only kid who understood him, and the cops still hadn't caught who did it. Campbell wondered if maybe he himself was the culprit. Maybe he had imagined going to shoot Roth, but had in fact bumped into Alex on the way there, and, stoned and half-crazy, had shot Alex by mistake, the bang! not registering until later. It was possible. Shit, anything was possible. Even heading off to a concert to kill Roth and his friends for dissing him at Alex's vigil a few weeks ago, and if those assholes weren't there, he had a long list of other assholes he could put out of their misery. After which (and this was the cool part), before blowing his own brains out, he was going to look at whoever was left standing and say, "Good luck with the new cat." Where the fuck did he get that from? They'd be trying to make sense of that comment for a very long time. Boom! Boom! Boom!

* * *

Barney was a few blocks from the town beach when he saw Campbell McVeigh out of the corner of his eye. He seemed to be walking with a purpose, pumping his arms and talking to himself, looking straight ahead and smiling. At what? Barney thought. Barney came to a stop and watched as Campbell disappeared into some pine trees near the cemetery. "Weird," he said to himself, then forgot about Campbell until he got to the next block where Campbell suddenly materialized in front of the car. Barney tried to stop, or at least he thought he did, but he couldn't be sure because everything went down so fast. Recognizing him, Campbell spread his legs, crouched, and pointed a gun at Barney. Whether Barney experienced the sound or the pain in his right shoulder first, he couldn't say, but the force of the entry wound made him lurch forward, his weight full on the accelerator. His last memory was of Campbell's awkward grin pressed against the windshield before he went tumbling over the top of the car. Unable to hold onto the wheel, Barney slumped forward, as the car rolled harmlessly forward until being stopped by a telephone pole. Through the rearview mirror, he could see Campbell's motionless body in the middle of the road. He was still holding onto the gun as blood began to pool around his head. Barney threw up onto his lap, and a very unpleasant possibility flashed through his mind. Maybe Campbell had shot at Barney because Barney had speeded up. If so, was this then a kind of murder? However you looked at it, Barney's life was about to change, though not in the way he expected, because, at that moment, slumped over in pain, with puke dripping from the steering wheel, he couldn't have known that Campbell had left a note on Facebook and Instagram about what he called "necessary casualties," or that, because of Barney, a lot of kids would sleep peacefully that night instead of being patched up by EMTs, or wheeled into the local morgue.

Barney Roth.

A hero.

Who would've ever expected that?

Acknowledgments

Some of these stories, or earlier versions of these stories, were previously published in the following periodicals or anthologies:

"X-Ray" in *Mississippi Review.*

"Flamenco" in *I'm a Man* by Peter Johnson (White Pine Press, 2003).

"The Gunslinger" in *Taking Aim: Power and Pain, Teens and Guns,* edited by Michael Cart (HarperCollins, 2015).

"Muscle" in *Bluestem.*

"Tail of the Comet" in *The Bryant Literary Review.*

"Pretty Girl" in *New World Writing.*

"Vigil" in *The Woven Tale Press.*

Special thanks to freelance editor Katya Rice for her fine editing and proofreading, and a nod to Catherine Liska for making a final pass at the manuscript.

About the Author

PETER JOHNSON's prose poetry and fiction have been awarded an NEA and two Rhode Island Council on the Arts fellowships. His second book of prose poems received the James Laughlin Award from The Academy of American Poets. New books are: *Old Man Howling at the Moon* (Madhat Press, 2018), *A Cast-Iron Aeroplane That Can Actually Fly: Commentaries from 80 Contemporary American Poets on Their Prose Poetry*, editor (MadHat Press, 2019), and *Truths, Falsehoods, and a Wee Bit of Honesty: A Short Primer on the Prose Poem, With Selected Letters from Russell Edson* (MadHat Press, 2020, just published). *Shot* is his second book of short stories, though he has written award-winning middle-grade and young adult fiction. He is at **peterjohnsonauthor.com**.